The Hooples' Horrible Holiday

Other Avon Camelot Books by
Stephen Manes

THE BOY WHO TURNED INTO A TV SET
HOOPLES ON THE HIGHWAY

STEPHEN MANES is a versatile and popular author and screen-writer. He has published more than twenty books for kids, including *The Hooples' Haunted House, Be a Perfect Person in Just Three Days!, That Game From Outer Space, The Oscar J. Noodleman Television Network,* and *Life Is No Fair!*. His column about humans and computers appears regularly in *PC Magazine*.

Mr. Manes lives in Riverdale, New York. When not writing with the help of a computer named Bambi, he is often found hiking, cross-country skiing, traveling, and overeating.

The Hooples' Horrible Holiday

STEPHEN MANES

Pictures by Wally Neibart

AN AVON CAMELOT BOOK

THE HOOPLES' HORRIBLE HOLIDAY is an original publication of Avon Books. This work has never before appeared in book form.

AVON BOOKS
A division of
The Hearst Corporation
1790 Broadway
New York, New York 10019

Library of Congress Cataloging in Publication Data

Manes, Stephen, 1949–
    Hooples' horrible holiday.
    (An Avon Camelot book)

    Summary: Alvin Hoople travels with his family to spend Thanksgiving at his grandparents' house, where a power failure and the most unusual turkey ever create a memorable holiday visit.
    [1. Thanksgiving Day—Fiction.   2. Grandparents— Fiction.   3. Family life—Fiction]   I. Title.
PZ7.M31264Hm   1986   [Fic]   86-7972

First Camelot Printing: November 1986

for Susan, fellow traveler

1

"Over the river and through the woods, to Grandmother's house we go," Alvin Hoople's little sister Annie chirped cheerfully.

Alvin made a face. At that very moment, he and his family weren't going anywhere at all. True, they were on the expressway to the airport, and they were already so close they could see planes taking off. But the car was stuck in the worst traffic jam Alvin had ever seen. It hadn't moved an inch in ten minutes.

"Over the river and through the woods," Annie sang for the twelfth time, "to Grandmother's house we go." She didn't know the rest of the words, and nobody was in the mood to teach her.

"If we don't start moving soon," muttered Mom, "we won't get to Grandmother's house for Thanksgiving at all. Our plane will take off, and we'll be down here looking up at it."

"Maybe that's our plane!" Annie said, pointing up at a jetliner soaring into the gray, drizzly skies.

"Don't be silly," said Alvin.

"How do you know?" Annie demanded.

Alvin checked his watch. "Our plane doesn't take off for an hour yet. Besides, that one's a 747. We're flying on a 727."

1

"Huh?" said Annie.

If there was one thing Alvin knew about, it was airplanes. He had airplane books and airplane mobiles and airplane models, and he could recognize almost any airliner just from its shape. "That one's a big plane," he explained. "We're flying on a medium-sized plane."

"I want to fly on a big plane!" Annie cried.

"Our plane will be plenty big enough for a shrimp like you."

"I am not a shrimp!" She put her nose against the wire window of the special "sky kennel" carrier on the seat beside her. "Right, Lambie?"

Lambie, the family cat, didn't say a word. "Lambie says I am not a shrimp," said Annie.

"Lambie's a shrimp himself," said Alvin.

"Pipe down, you two, or you're both going to be shrimp cocktail!" Dad declared. "I want to hear this traffic report."

"Let's check it out with the latest from our eye in the sky," said the announcer.

"I don't see any eyes up there," said Annie.

"Shhh," said Mom.

"We're in the trafficopter over the airport expressway right now, and there's nothing 'express' about it," reported a distant voice, with whirring noises in the background. "As usual for the holiday getaway, this airport traffic's our worst bottleneck. They're backed up out here for two miles from the city and one mile from the suburbs."

"Well, it could be worse," Dad sighed. "We could be coming from the city."

"It's just one big parking lot down there," the voice on the radio announced cheerfully. "The airport is now advising travelers to allow at least one extra hour to reach their flights."

Dad grunted, shook his head, and turned off the radio.

"What if we miss the plane?" Alvin wondered.

"Don't even think about it," said Dad.

But when anybody told Alvin not to think about something, that something suddenly filled his brain. They just couldn't miss their plane! It would ruin absolutely everything!

Thanksgiving had always been one of Alvin's all-time favorite holidays. The only thing wrong with Thanksgiving was that it didn't come with presents. But it did mean two days off from school instead of just one. It meant a big family get-together. And it meant food that made Alvin drool just to think about it.

Even though the November page of his Baseball Greats calendar had a big picture of Hank Aaron, it never reminded Alvin of home runs. Every time he saw that magic word *November,* Alvin thought about wolfing down turkey and stuffing and cranberry sauce and mashed potatoes and gravy and pumpkin pie and ice cream until he was so stuffed he could barely move. When his teacher asked the class to write about the meaning of Thanksgiving, Alvin was tempted to put down that Thanksgiving was the holiday when humans give thanks for being stuffed but turkeys don't.

And this particular Thanksgiving was going to be extra special. Usually Mom's parents, the Montoons, otherwise known as Grandma and Gramps, came to Alvin's house. Two years ago everybody had gone to his cousin Marty's house outside Philadelphia. But this year they would all be celebrating Thanksgiving at his grandparents' place in Tyler, Illinois.

Better still, Alvin was going to get there by taking his first real airplane ride. Mom and Dad claimed Alvin had flown when he was six weeks old, but he didn't remember that at all, so it didn't really count. This time he wasn't about to forget. He knew all the flight information by heart: Falcon Airways flight 662, Boeing 727, dinner service, departing Buffalo 5:05 P.M., arriving Chicago, Illinois, 5:46 P.M. It sounded like a short flight, but it would actually take an hour longer than

Alvin first suspected, because Chicago was in the central time zone and it would really be 6:46 Sherwood Forest time when they landed.

Alvin looked at his watch. There were still fifty-five minutes left until the plane was due to take off. He looked at the traffic up ahead. It was barely moving.

With a roar that made Annie put her hands over her ears, a big plane zoomed into the air right above the Hooples' car. Alvin wished he were on that plane right now. It might not be going to the right place, but at least it was going *somewhere*. And that was more than he could say about the car.

Alvin tried not to think about what would happen if they missed their plane. He thought back to that morning, when he'd been roped into playing the turkey in the school pageant because the original turkey had come down with chicken pox. It was kind of embarrassing in a way, but his friends said he'd done a great job of gobbling around.

Backstage afterward, everybody talked about Thanksgiving. Some kids were going to visit their relatives, and some kids' relatives were going to visit them, and some kids were going to stay home alone with their parents. Some were going to football games, and some were going to parades. But there was one thing they all had in common. Everybody was going to be eating turkey.

Well, almost everybody. Cindy, the vegetarian, said her family would be having bean casserole. Nobody else could believe it; Thanksgiving without turkey would be like Halloween without candy or April Fools' Day without somebody telling you your shoelace was untied. But Cindy said it was mean to kill a big old bird just to eat it, and besides, she was going to have a giant chocolate cake in the shape of the *Mayflower,* which was a whole lot better. Alvin agreed it sounded a whole lot better than the beans.

4

But the way things were going, he was beginning to think he might be lucky to get a few beans for Thanksgiving dinner. Planes were taking off and landing all around; cars were going nowhere. Alvin wished his family had a car that could turn into a helicopter like the one he'd read about in a book about transportation of the future.

He looked at his watch: still fifty minutes left. They could probably get there in time if they hurried. But how could you hurry when every car on the road was standing still?

Suddenly the Hooples' car began to roll forward again. "Rubberneckers!" Dad snorted. "Everybody slowed down to look at this accident."

Alvin took a look for himself as they drove past. The front of a cookie truck was bashed in, and the rear bumper of a long black limousine was all crumpled up. Fortunately, nobody seemed to be hurt.

Better still, the Hooples were almost there! The car zipped right underneath a sign that said AIRPORT PARKING.

"Hooray!" Dad shouted.

"Hoorah!" Mom yelled.

"Oh, boy!" Alvin hollered.

"Wait! We have to go back!" Annie cried.

Nobody said a word. The car came to a stop at a red light.

"I left Lambie's catnip mouse at home!" Annie wailed.

"Too bad!" Alvin snapped.

"He won't have any fun this whole vacation!" Annie insisted.

"He will too!" said Alvin.

"We'll buy him a new mouse," Mom offered.

"It's not the same," Annie declared.

Nobody answered her.

"Mom!" Annie pleaded.

The light turned green. The car pulled forward.

5

"Dad!" Annie wailed.

"Nobody will have any fun at all if we don't get on that plane," Dad said. "End of discussion."

Annie wrinkled her nose and whispered to Lambie that she'd done the best she could.

Dad leaned out the window to take a ticket from a machine, and a striped wooden bar went up to let the car in. Alvin looked at his watch. There were forty-five minutes to spare.

They'd be able to make their flight after all! Alvin was sure of it!

2

The airport parking lot was enormous. It was almost as big as the one at the mall. There was just one minor problem. Every last space was taken. The lot was so crowded people had even parked in places marked NO PARKING. Dad was so frustrated he muttered a couple of words Alvin wasn't allowed to.

"Would you repeat that?" Alvin asked.

"Never mind," said Mom.

"There are no spaces *anywhere*," Dad grumbled. "Keep your eyes peeled, everybody."

"There's a space!" Annie pointed out the window. "It's a really good one!"

And it would have been, too, except for a few signs along the fence in front of it. The signs read NO PARKING, TOW-AWAY ZONE, KEEP CLEAR, DRIVEWAY, and EMERGENCY DRIVEWAY—DO NOT BLOCK. Dad kept driving.

"What's wrong with that space?" Annie wondered.

"See those signs?" Alvin asked.

"Of course I can see those signs," said Annie.

"Well, they all say NO PARKING," Alvin told her.

Annie pouted. "I knew that."

"We've only got forty minutes to get to the plane," Mom said. "What are we going to do?"

"I think I am going to have to park illegally," said Dad.

"You're going to break the law?" Alvin asked. He had never before heard his father even suggest such a thing.

"As terrible as it might seem, that is just what I may have to do."

"Don't do it!" Annie shrieked. "They'll put you in jail!"

"More likely they'll put the car in jail," Mom said. "They might bring a tow truck and haul it away."

"Or they might give us a ticket," said Alvin.

"Wait a minute!" Mom cried. "Stop!"

Dad pulled up in front of a blue-and-white police car that was patrolling the lot. "Excuse me," Mom said, leaning out the window. "We're late for our plane, and we can't find a place to park anywhere."

"You're not the only ones," said the policeman as though he'd heard this story many times before. "This happens every Thanksgiving."

"What should we do?" Mom asked.

"Park anywhere. As long as you don't block anyone from getting out or park where it says NO PARKING, you'll be okay."

"We won't get a ticket?" Alvin asked.

"Not unless we find the car where it's causing trouble—and then we'll tow it away."

Mom thanked the policeman, and eventually Alvin spotted a narrow space. Dad parked very carefully and told everyone to make sure not to scratch the other cars on the way out. "Now come on, everybody," he said. "Shake a leg."

Alvin stuck his leg out his door and shook it. Annie giggled.

"Alvin, we don't have time for foolishness," Mom said. "We're going to be lucky if we get on that plane at all."

Alvin checked his watch. "We still have twenty-eight minutes," he said.

"And we're going to need every last one of them," Dad replied. "Now help me with this luggage."

"Seven!" Annie cried, pointing to a sign over the row where they were parked. "That's a seven!"

"Very good," said Mom.

"Seven!" Annie shouted again. "One more than six!" Annie's favorite TV show was *Sesame Street*.

One more than two minutes later, everybody had his hands full. Dad and Mom took the biggest suitcases, along with a shopping bag or two. Annie carried Lambie's kennel in one hand and held on to Dad's hand with the other. As for Alvin, he was in charge of two carry-on bags that dangled from shoulder straps, and a bakery box with a fancy holiday cake Mom had bought. "Remember, keep it upright," she told him. "We don't want it to turn into an upside-down cake."

"Right!" Alvin said, wondering if there was any way he could sneak a pinkie in and get a lick of icing later on.

"To the terminal, and quick!" Dad declared.

Light drizzle was still falling. "What about our umbrellas?" Annie wondered.

"We don't have enough hands for umbrellas," Dad said. "A little rain won't melt you. Just hurry." But loaded down with luggage, cakes, cats, and Annies, no one could go much faster than a sort of waddle.

The terminal was way down at the other end of the parking lot. It didn't seem fair. Just getting to the plane might end up taking longer than the flight itself. And the luggage seemed to get heavier with every step. By the time he spotted the FALCON AIRWAYS sign, Alvin thought his shoulders might drop off.

Dad led everybody into the terminal through big glass doors that opened automatically. He stopped at the end of a long line of people and luggage that led

9

to a counter marked TICKETED PASSENGERS CHECK BAG-GAGE. With a sigh of relief, the Hooples set their bags down on the floor.

Alvin looked up at two TV screens above the counter. He found the important information on the fourth line of the DEPARTURES display. It said FLIGHT 662—CHICAGO—5:05—42. Forty-two was the gate number. And right beside it were the words ON TIME.

Alvin's watch said 4:47. The line of passengers was moving even slower than the expressway traffic. If it didn't speed up soon, they'd never make it on time.

"Uh-oh," said Dad. "Who has the tickets?"

"You do," said Mom.

Dad frowned. "I thought you did."

Mom rummaged through her purse. Dad looked in his coat. No tickets. Mom looked in her carry-on bag, and Dad looked in his briefcase. No tickets anywhere.

"Great!" Alvin muttered.

"They have to be somewhere," said Mom.

Alvin pointed to something sticking out of his father's shirt pocket. "What's that?"

Dad shook his head sheepishly. "Tickets. Precisely where I put them."

"Anybody here with departure times before five-thirty?" called out a woman at a second counter.

Somebody at the front of the line cried out, "Here!" Dad waved the tickets in the air and shouted, "Us!" The woman gestured for them to come ahead.

At exactly 4:51 by Alvin's digital watch, Dad handed the tickets to the woman at the counter and lifted the biggest suitcases onto a little platform. The woman put tags on each handle and handed the tickets back. Then Dad divided up the bags that were left and led the way around the counter and down a corridor marked GATES 30–48.

It was the longest hallway Alvin had ever seen. It was so long it had a big rubber conveyor belt to carry people part of the way. You could stand and just let the belt whisk you along, or you could walk at superhuman speed, which is what Alvin wanted to do. But he had to stand with the rest of his family, since that's what everybody in front of them was doing. "It's a human traffic jam," Alvin griped.

But when he looked ahead, he spotted something even worse. "Oh, no! Another line!"

"Now you know why they call them airlines," Dad joked without cracking a smile. Up ahead, people who had gotten off the moving walkway were waiting in line to put their baggage on a smaller conveyor belt or waiting in a second line to step through a little doorway. Dad explained that the baggage was being X-rayed to check for bombs or guns. The doorway, Mom said, was a metal detector that checked for the same things on people's bodies.

Alvin checked his watch. There were just ten minutes left till departure time. But at least the line was moving quickly. Mom put her bag on the belt and told Alvin to put the box there, too. Dad handed Lambie's carrier to a uniformed woman beside the doorway, and she looked inside while Dad walked through. Then Annie and Mom stepped through the doorway. Finally it was Alvin's turn.

Brrzap! A loud buzzer went off in the doorway. Alvin felt terribly embarrassed.

"Put all your coins, keys, and other metal objects in this tray," said the guard.

"And hurry!" said Dad.

Alvin reached into his pockets and dumped his keys and all his change in the tray. "Walk around the detector, then come through again," said the guard. Alvin followed her instructions.

Brzzaapp! He'd done it again! The guard scowled at him, and so did Mom and Dad. Annie giggled as though it were the funniest thing she'd ever seen. Alvin felt horrible.

"You didn't forget your pocketknife or something, did you?" asked the guard.

Alvin fished around in his pockets and came up with his wallet. Then he remembered his metal comb, the one he'd gotten for his birthday. "Put them in the tray and try again," the guard said wearily.

The people in line behind the doorway were beginning to get impatient. Alvin blushed bright red as he went through for the third time.

This time he passed the test, and a few of the people in line applauded sarcastically. Alvin put his comb back in his pocket, and then his keys. But when he grabbed his change, a quarter clattered to the floor and rolled under the baggage-inspection machine. Alvin reached underneath, but all he found was a dried-up piece of used bubble gum.

"Come on!" said Mom. "And take the cake!"

"But I lost a quarter," Alvin said. "It might be my lucky quarter, the one from the year I was born."

"If we don't get moving, that's not all you'll lose," said Dad.

Alvin snatched the cake box from the conveyor belt and looked at a clock on the wall. They had exactly four minutes to get to gate 42. But they were only at gate 30, and the hallway ahead seemed to stretch on forever.

"Hurry!" Dad cried, picking up Annie and tucking her under one arm like a football. "We might still make it!"

The Hooples scrambled down the corridor as though they were running for their lives. Alvin kept a close watch on the gates, which didn't look like gates at all. They were more like big waiting rooms with lots of chairs full of people. Dodging oncoming passengers and luggage carts, the Hooples dashed past gates 30 and 31, 32 and 33, a big snack bar, a magazine stand, a gift shop, a bunch of rest rooms, and gates 34 and 35 and 36 and 37. Finally they came to a big circular room

12

where the gates went all around. Alvin spotted a big number 42 over a counter to the left.

Dad set Annie down and dashed up to the counter with Alvin right behind him. "Flight 662?" Dad panted.

"Well..." said the man behind the counter as Dad handed him the tickets.

"Are we on time?" Alvin interrupted, out of breath.

The gate clerk looked at his watch. "Almost."

"Uh-oh," said Mom.

"But you're in luck," said the clerk. "Your flight is approximately forty-five minutes late."

"The TV screens say it's on time," Alvin said.

"The TV screens are all out of whack," said the clerk. "Our computer is down." He looked at the tickets and handed them back to Dad. "Your flight is now departing at five-fifty from gate thirty."

"All the way back there?" Alvin asked.

"Don't worry," replied the clerk. "You have plenty of time."

"Better late than never, I guess," said Dad.

Alvin caught his breath and checked through his pockets. It was just as he'd suspected. He had lots of plain old regular coins in his pocket, but his lucky quarter had vanished.

"Carry me some more!" Annie said, tugging at Dad's jacket. "That was better than a piggyback ride!"

"I think your father is a wee bit worn out," said Mom. "How about using your own two feet?"

"Okay," said Annie. "But what are we going to do now?"

"I don't know about everybody else," said Alvin, "but I'm going to look for my lucky quarter."

3

Alvin knew it was silly to be superstitious. He didn't mind walking under ladders, and he didn't worry about what happened on Friday the Thirteenth. But his grandfather had given him the lucky quarter when he was about Annie's age, and Gramps had said, "As long as you have this, you'll never be broke." Alvin had carried it with him everywhere ever since.

But now, he thought as the Hooples trudged back down the corridor, it might be gone forever. What would Gramps say if he found out?

"That girl has a Carly Cutie doll!" Annie cried, loud enough for half the airport to hear. Alvin winced. From all the talk about Carly Cutie dolls at breakfast, lunch, dinner, and between-meal snacks, Alvin was positive Annie would be unwrapping one of the ugly babies on Christmas morning. Why any sane human being would want such a thing totally baffled him.

"Hello, Carly Cutie!" Annie called out to the entire gate 36 waiting area as she waved to the doll. Its cute little redheaded owner waved the doll's hand back and brought the doll over to Annie.

"Carly Cutie says hello," said the girl with the doll.

"Hello, Carly Cutie," said Annie.

It was just too cute for Alvin to stand. Besides, he had important things to do. "Come on, Annie," he said. "We can't stand around here looking at dumb dolls. I've got to find my lucky quarter."

Annie didn't seem to hear. "You really are cute," Annie told the doll.

"Come on, Dad," Alvin urged. "I want to get back there before somebody steals my lucky quarter. Tell Annie not to slow us down." But Dad and Mom didn't seem to be in any particular hurry.

"I have a Carly Cutie doll, and you-oo-ou don't!" sang Annie's new acquaintance. She made a face and stuck out her tongue to emphasize the point.

"Big deal," said Annie. "I have a Care Bears doll and a Cabbage Patch Kid and a talking teddy bear and—"

"Carly Cutie says that stuff is for little kids."

"I say Carly Cutie should shut up before I give her a poke in the nose," said Annie.

"Mom! That little girl wants to hit my doll!" Carly Cutie's redheaded friend cried, and then ran back to her mother.

"And I'm not little!" Annie hollered. "I'm bigger than you are!"

The redheaded girl's mother gave Mom and Dad a dirty look.

"Annie, I think we should get moving," said Dad.

"Okay," said Annie. "I guess I showed *her!*" And the Hooples started down the corridor again. Alvin just hoped his lucky quarter hadn't disappeared for good.

Though he still loved airplanes, Alvin was beginning to think airports were kind of boring. There wasn't much to do but walk down long corridors or sit in smoky waiting areas. Even the snack bar looked rather unappetizing. And the gift shop seemed to specialize in junky souvenirs and toys you wouldn't give your worst enemy.

16

But on a table right at the front of the gift shop was a special display that captured Annie's eye before Alvin knew what was happening. "It's Carly Cutie!" she shrieked.

In a flash, Annie ran toward the gift shop, snatched the box from the table, and cradled it in her arms. She stared at the doll as though it were her very own daughter. "Dad, buy me this," she begged. Alvin was sure his lucky quarter was doomed.

"We have to get down to our gate now," said Dad.

"Right after you buy me this."

"Annie, I think you'd better put that back."

Dad reached for the box, but Annie pulled it away and clutched it tighter. "Annie, come on," said Mom. "Put it back."

"This is Carly Cutie and I love her and she is going to fly to Grandma's with me."

"Wrong," said Dad, exasperated. "Ann L. Hoople is going to fly to Grandma's with Lambie and the rest of her family. Carly Cutie will have to stay here, because Carly Cutie doesn't have a ticket." He reached for the box, but Annie whirled away from him.

"I'll buy her a ticket," said Annie.

"Fine," said Dad. "It will cost you one hundred and fifty dollars each way."

"Oh," said Annie.

"Now maybe you'd like to say good-bye to Carly Cutie and put her back where she belongs."

"No, I wouldn't." Annie pouted.

"Well, I suppose we could take Carly Cutie with us to Grandma's and leave you behind," said Mom.

Annie thought it over. "Maybe I'll see you at Christmas," she told the doll as she put it back on the table and sadly waved good-bye.

"Now can we go look for my quarter?" Alvin asked.

"As soon as we get settled in at the gate," said Dad.

But the gate 30 waiting area was completely full.

17

Fortunately, Mom managed to scrounge up four seats near the window of gate 32 right next door. Dad and Alvin left her with Annie and the luggage and hurried back to the security area.

While he waited politely to ask the woman at the X-ray machine if she'd seen his lucky quarter, Alvin looked over her shoulder. A little television screen showed the insides of people's luggage. Alvin was hoping he'd spot some interesting hijacker's stuff, like a gun or a long knife, but the only thing that came close was an umbrella.

Worse, his lucky quarter was nowhere to be found. The woman at the X-ray machine hadn't seen it, and neither had any of the guards.

"I'm sure it's under there," said Alvin. "Can't you move the machine or something?"

"Afraid not," said one of the guards. "It's bolted to the floor."

"Well, thanks anyway," said Alvin, very discouraged. Losing a lucky quarter would have been bad enough anytime. But losing it at the very beginning of Thanksgiving vacation seemed to foretell a terrible doom.

Dad dug down into his pocket and came up with a fistful of change. He looked at the dates on the quarters and handed one to Alvin.

Alvin looked at it. "This isn't from the year I was born."

"No," said Dad. "It's from the year Annie was born."

"What good is that?"

"Well, it's better than a bucket of warm spit."

Alvin laughed. Every now and then his father came up with things that parents weren't supposed to say at all.

"And," Dad added, "it comes with extra-special luck built right in. If you take it to any bank, you can exchange it for twenty-five genuine copper medallions of our nation's sixteenth president."

Alvin smiled. When you looked at it that way, a lucky quarter from the year Annie was born didn't seem so terrible. After all, as long as he had it, he'd never be broke.

4

There wasn't much to see from the window of the waiting area. Now and then a man on the ground would use funny-looking paddles to guide a plane up to a gate. Then a jetway, a sort of hallway on wheels, would roll up to the plane to let people out. And Alvin saw little trucks drive up to waiting planes and load them with big metal boxes full of luggage or food. But most of the time there was nothing new to look at except people in the windows across the way looking back at him.

Then he spotted a plane taxiing right past the window. He could actually see the pilot and copilot in the cockpit as it headed for gate 30.

"Is this our plane?" Alvin wondered.

"Sure looks like it," Dad said.

"Let's go!" Annie said, looking up from her coloring book, where she had given Snow White a purple face.

"Not so fast," said Mom. "The people on it have to get out first."

Out they came: men in suits, women in dresses, kids in jeans, virtually everyone lugging a suitcase or a briefcase or a shopping bag or a bunch of clothes on hangers. Finally the captain and crew stepped off the plane in black uniforms with gold braid on the caps.

"Shouldn't be long now," said Mom.

And it wasn't. "Welcome to Falcon Airways flight 662, now ready for preboarding," said a voice over a crackly loudspeaker. "At this time, we ask passengers with small children or special boarding problems to please appear at the gate."

"Well, between Annie and Lambie we've got a small child and a special boarding problem, so I guess that means us," said Mom.

The Hooples gathered all their belongings and walked to the door with the big 30 over it. "Three-oh!" Annie called out as Dad showed a woman the boarding passes and led the way through the door. Alvin was disappointed to discover that the jetway looked exactly like a plain old hallway except for a couple of control panels marked DANGER.

But the minute he stepped aboard the airplane, Alvin got excited again. The door to the cockpit was partway open, and Alvin could see all the knobs and dials and digital readouts the pilots used.

"Welcome aboard," said a man with a handlebar moustache and a blue sport jacket that said *Falcon Airways* on the pocket. "May I see your boarding passes?"

Dad handed them over.

"Do you drive the plane?" Annie asked.

"No, sweetheart, I don't. I'm a flight attendant," the mustachioed man said with a smile. "Mostly what I do is serve your drinks and your meal."

"I'd like a hamburger and a root beer, please!" said Annie.

"It doesn't work quite that way. Your folks will explain it to you." He handed the boarding passes back to Dad. "You're all in row eight. Seats A, C, D, and E."

"He doesn't know his alphabet!" Annie whispered to Alvin.

"I heard that!" said the flight attendant. "It just so happens that there are no seats with the letter *B* on this plane."

21

"How come?" Alvin asked.

"If you knew how many times people ask that question!" The flight attendant laughed. "It's supposed to have something to do with the computer."

"Maybe the computer doesn't know the alphabet," Mom joked.

"Considering how often it breaks down, I wouldn't be a bit surprised."

"Can I see the cockpit?" Alvin asked.

"It's impossible right now," the flight attendant replied, "because we're running so far behind schedule. Maybe when we land the captain will let you take a peek."

A line was beginning to form in the jetway behind them. "Come on, kids," Dad said, leading them up the aisle.

Little signs above the windows marked each row of seats. The flight attendant was right: the three seats on the left side of each row were marked D, E, and F, but the seats on the right were labeled A and C. B had mysteriously vanished.

"Who sits where?" Mom asked.

"Lambie sits with me," said Annie. "Right, Lambie?"

"I want a window," said Alvin.

"Me, too," said Annie.

"Alvin asked first," said Dad. "Alvin, you're in A. I'll sit in C. Alice, you've got D, and Annie has E."

"I want the window over there," said Annie.

"Somebody else has seat F," said Mom.

"But I want it," said Annie.

Dad gave Alvin one of his "wouldn't you like to be nice to your little sister?" looks. But Alvin really did want a window seat, and he thought Annie was just being ornery. "I did ask first," he said.

Dad nodded, riffled through the boarding passes, and handed one to Annie. "Annie," he said, "this is your ticket. Can you read it?"

Annie nodded. "Every word," she lied.

Dad pointed. "Tell me what it says right there."

Annie looked closely, then thought it over to make sure. "Eight. E."

"Very good," said Dad. "And here, Miss Ann L. Hoople, is seat eight E. This is your seat. Please sit down in it."

"Okay," said Annie, half smiling and half frowning.

"Thank you," said Dad.

"Wow! It's got a seat belt!" said Annie. "This is okay!"

Alvin thought so, too. The seats were tall and comfortable, and they tilted back like Dad's recliner at home. Above were lighted signs that said FASTEN SEAT BELT and NO SMOKING, and cupboards where Dad stuffed the coats and some of the shopping bags. Lambie's cage went under the seat in front of Annie with a stern warning from Mom about leaving it closed. And Alvin fit the cake under the seat in front of him with plenty of room to spare.

The kangaroo-style pouch in the back of that seat was full of neat stuff: a plastic card with information on what to do in case of emergency, a catalog full of expensive gifts that all said *Falcon Airways* on them, and a magazine called *Falcon Flight* with articles on Dayton, Ohio, and Harrisburg, Pennsylvania, and a special Thanksgiving feature on turkey raising. There was also a little paper bag that said IN CASE OF MOTION SICKNESS. Apparently Annie had one of her own, because Alvin heard her ask, "What's this little bag for?"

The armrest had little buttons on it. Alvin pressed one with the picture of a light bulb, and a reading lamp high overhead went on and off. But when he pressed a button with a picture of a woman, nothing happened at all.

"What's that button for?" Alvin asked.

"Used to be to call the flight attendants if you needed something," said Dad. "It'd make a little *bong* and light

23

up a special light above your seat. But mostly they're disconnected now. Some passengers used to drive everybody crazy with the bonging."

Alvin noticed the parade of people, shopping bags, and luggage stumbling down the aisle. "How long till we take off?" he wondered.

"Just as soon as everybody gets aboard," Dad said. "It shouldn't be long now."

Alvin noticed a large man in a business suit and tie stuffing his coat into one of the cupboards across the aisle. The man looked down in Mom's direction and pointed toward the window. Then he climbed over Mom and Annie and plopped down in seat 8F.

"Hi," said Annie.

"Hello," said her new seatmate gruffly.

"This is Lambie," Annie said.

"Lambie?" The man grunted. "Next thing you know, they'll be letting hogs and cows on the plane."

"Lambie is my kitty," Annie explained.

"Well, I suppose that's better," said Annie's seatmate. "But I thought they didn't allow animals in the passenger cabin."

"One per flight," Mom informed him.

"Must be my lucky day," Annie's seatmate replied. He turned to look out the window.

"That man's not very friendly," Annie said. Mom put her finger to her lips to shush Annie up.

Suddenly there was a lurch, and the plane started moving backward. Alvin looked out the window. The plane was slowly rolling away from the terminal.

"Good afternoon, Chicago passengers," said a voice over the loudspeakers. Alvin paid close attention to a woman in a flight attendant's jacket who reminded him of his old third-grade teacher. She demonstrated how to fasten your seat belt and how the little yellow oxygen masks would drop down from above if the cabin lost pressure.

24

"Were you ever in a plane when the oxygen masks came down?" Alvin asked his father.

"Nope," Dad admitted. "And I don't plan to start now."

Then the woman explained that the seat cushions floated so you could use them in an emergency landing on water. She said further instructions were on the card in the seat pocket.

Alvin looked at the card. It was almost all pictures. There was a picture of the seat belt, there was a picture of a cigarette in a red circle with a red slash over it, there was a picture of how to open the emergency doors and jump down to the slide, and there was even a picture of how to yank the cushions from the seats.

"Did you ever do any of these things?" Alvin asked Dad.

"Yes. On every single flight."

Alvin brightened. "Really?"

"Yes. I fastened my seat belt. And I didn't smoke in the aisles or in the bathroom. Or anywhere else, for that matter."

Alvin frowned. "Dad, you know what I mean...."

Dad shook his head. "No. I've never been in anything even close to an emergency situation. It doesn't happen often, which is a very good thing."

Alvin wondered what an emergency would be like and whether he'd be able to save everybody because he now knew how to open the doors and jump down the slide. But he wasn't in the mood for a real emergency this time around. He suspected it might get in the way of Thanksgiving dinner.

A different woman's voice came over the loud-speaker. "This is the captain speaking. We are cleared to enter the main runway, and we will be taking off momentarily."

Alvin looked out the window and saw a plane landing in the distance. Then his own plane made a wide turn onto the main runway. The engines on the wings beneath his window began to roar, and his seat began to vibrate. The plane rolled forward faster and faster, and the wings bounced up and down.

Suddenly Alvin felt the plane tilt back. The wings stopped bouncing, and the ride turned smoother, and the ground got further and further away.

The plane was in the air! He was actually flying! Next stop, Chicago!

5

Alvin watched trees and cars and houses and roads get smaller and smaller below as the plane soared into the air. Then the plane climbed into the middle of thick gray clouds. Everything else disappeared except raindrops that moved sideways along the windows. But Alvin thought he saw the clouds becoming brighter, and a second later the plane broke through the cloudtops into blue sky and bright sun.

It was beautiful. Below, in all directions, was a sea of billowy white clouds. Rain was only for earthbound folks. Alvin pretended he was king of the clouds. He'd live up here in the sunlight and drench the humans below now and then just for amusement.

Then with a loud *bong!*, the NO SMOKING and FASTEN SEAT BELT lights went off, and the woman who looked like his third-grade teacher made an announcement, saying that you were free to move about the cabin but that it was a good idea to leave your seat belt fastened when you were sitting down. The captain's voice crackled over the loudspeaker. She apologized for the delay, and said it would be cloudy all the way to Chicago, and that the air temperature outside the cabin was a chilly thirty degrees below zero Fahrenheit. The plane was just outside Cleveland, Ohio, at an altitude of 26,000 feet.

"How many miles up is that?" Alvin wondered.

"There are 5,280 feet in a mile," said Dad. "Divide 26,000 by 5,280 and see what you get."

"My calculator's at home," Alvin replied.

"You can do it in your head."

"Maybe *you* can," said Alvin.

"Five miles, more or less."

"Wow! Five miles! That's a long way down."

"Don't jump without your parachute. Or with it."

Alvin noticed Mom and Annie popping out of their seats and heading toward the back of the plane.

"A-i-r-s-i-c-k?" Dad spelled to Mom.

"No, thank heaven. Just a routine visit."

"Come on!" Annie urged. Mom led the way.

Alvin felt slightly jealous. The idea of going to the bathroom five miles up suddenly appealed to him. He unfastened his seat belt and stood up. "I think I'll go, too," he said.

"Hold your horses," said Dad. "There are only two bathrooms on this plane, and people whose name doesn't happen to be Hoople just might want to use one of them."

"But I have to go," said Alvin. Actually, he didn't. He was just extremely curious about what an airplane bathroom would look like.

"As soon as Mom and Annie get back," Dad said.

Alvin impatiently looked out the window at the sky and the clouds, but the view hadn't changed much. He looked at the free magazine, which was full of ads for rental cars and a club you could join that would give you a free flight every ten times you flew on Falcon Airways. Alvin thought of sending in the postcard and joining, but considering how much he traveled, he'd be something like thirty years old before he got his first free flight, and he decided that wasn't worth the stamp.

Finally Annie and Mom returned. Alvin climbed over

his father and walked down the aisle toward the back. A smelly blue haze hung in the air. The rear section was for smokers, and they all must have lit up the moment the sign had been turned off. Alvin felt as though he would start coughing any second.

Then he noticed the LAVATORY signs and the two blank doors at the back. Neither one said MEN—or WOMEN, for that matter. Neither one had a picture of a man or a woman or even ROMEOS and JULIETS like the bathrooms at his parents' favorite Italian restaurant. Alvin decided that it didn't matter which bathroom he used.

He turned the doorknob on the left. The door didn't open, and an irritated man shouted, "Read the sign!" from inside. Then Alvin noticed that the door had a little window with the word OCCUPIED in it. So did the one on the right.

Alvin waited patiently and hoped he wouldn't die from the smoke. Then a woman came out the right-hand door, excused herself, and brushed past him. Alvin looked at the little sign. It now said VACANT. He turned the doorknob and went in.

It was just like a real bathroom, only smaller. On one side were a big mirror, a box of tissues, a roll of toilet paper, a paper-towel dispenser, a NO SMOKING sign, a metal sink with a little round basin, and a place to plug your electric shaver. When he slid the little knob on the door to lock it, extra lights went on over the sink.

Alvin decided to wash his hands. A little compartment was full of tiny soaps like the ones he remembered from motels. He took one and unwrapped it.

The faucets had little levers marked H and C, but the water stopped the instant you let go of them. Alvin guessed that helped save water, but it also made it hard to wash his hands under running water the way he liked to.

He filled up the little basin and washed his hands. He pushed another lever, and the dirty water disappeared down the drain with the kind of slurping noise you make with a straw when you're down to the bottom of your glass. He rinsed his hands one at a time, dried them on a paper towel, and tossed the towel through the door marked TOWEL DISPOSAL—DO NOT PUT TOWELS IN TOILET.

Then he realized he hadn't checked out the toilet. The water inside was dyed dark blue. Alvin pressed a little button on the wall beside a sign that said TOILET FLUSH.

Just as Alvin expected, more blue water came down the sides of the toilet bowl. There was just one problem: it wouldn't stop.

Alvin thought the little button might be stuck, so he tried to pull it out. It didn't move. Then the whole plane began to bounce around, and the blue water began sloshing in the bowl.

The water was getting closer and closer to the top. Alvin tried pushing the button again. Nothing happened. The blue water kept climbing higher.

Alvin turned the doorknob, but the door wouldn't budge. Then a little sign by the door started flashing. RETURN TO CABIN, it said.

"We are encountering some turbulence," squawked a woman's voice through the loudspeaker. "Please return to your seat and fasten your seat belt."

There wasn't anything Alvin would have rather done at that moment. The voice wasn't kidding about needing a seat belt. Alvin felt a dip like the ones he remembered from the Deadly Drop roller coaster he'd been on last summer.

The blue water sloshed over the bowl and onto the floor. Alvin just hoped it wouldn't mess up his shoes. He still couldn't open the door.

"Help!" he cried.

"What's the trouble?" said a voice outside.

"The toilet's overflowing and I'm stuck in here!"

30

"Just slide it open," said the voice.

Alvin stood on tiptoe to avoid the blue water. He grabbed the doorknob to keep from falling as the plane lurched back and forth. He didn't see anything to slide open on the toilet. "What?" he said.

"The door. Just slide the lock open."

"Oh," Alvin said. He looked up and slid the little lock button to the left. Then he turned the doorknob and stepped outside. A little of the blue water followed him.

"What a mess," said the man outside. "Shut the door, quick. I've got to get back to my seat." And he disappeared up the aisle.

Alvin shut the door and grabbed a handy handle on the wall to steady himself. Blue water trickled under the door.

An elderly woman came out of the other bathroom and nearly stepped in the puddle. "Watch out!" said Alvin.

The woman tiptoed around the water. "What happened?" she asked.

"The toilet overflowed."

"Oh," said the woman, giving Alvin a very dirty look that made it clear she was sure it was all his fault.

The flight attendant with the moustache arrived, took one look, and shook his head. "Did you put paper towels in that toilet?"

"I didn't put anything in there!" Alvin said.

"I'll *bet* you didn't."

"I didn't! Honest!" said Alvin.

"All right," said the flight attendant. "Just get back to your seat. You're not supposed to be out here when the seat-belt sign is on."

"It wasn't my fault," Alvin said, and started up the aisle.

The woman who looked like Alvin's third-grade teacher brushed past Alvin to help. "Kids!" Alvin heard the male flight attendant mutter behind him. "We shouldn't give them a special discount fare! We should charge them double!"

Alvin wanted to protest, but he saw his father waving to him ahead. And Alvin was having trouble enough just getting back to his seat. The plane was bouncing up and down and sideways, and Alvin had to grab the side of each seat as he made his way up the aisle. It was kind of like walking on the back of a bucking bronco. In fact, when Alvin finally reached his row, he saw Annie going "Yippee! Ride 'em, cowboy!" across the aisle. The man next to her was shaking his head.

"Where have you been?" Mom asked Alvin.

"We thought you fell out or something," Dad said as Alvin climbed over him and buckled himself in. "What happened back there?"

"You wouldn't believe," was all Alvin could say.

Mom leaned across the aisle toward Dad. "Guess what?" she said, gesturing toward Annie.

"I'm carsick," Annie said.

Mom opened the bag and handed it to her. "You mean you're airsick."

"No," said Annie. "I'm carsick! I'm nauseous! I'm going to throw up!"

Her seatmate put his hands over his eyes as though he couldn't bear to look.

6

The turbulence stopped as quickly as it had started, and Annie didn't throw up at all. In fact, she heard the magic words "root beer" and made a miraculous recovery.

The flight attendants were wheeling carts down the aisle and offering free sodas and packets of peanuts that you could eat on a little table that dropped down from the seat in front of you. You could also buy cute little bottles of liquor if you were old enough. Dad and Mom didn't get any, but Alvin noticed that Annie's seatmate ordered three.

As he drank his soda Alvin watched a dazzling sunset above the clouds. Then it turned dark out, and Alvin could see only the lights flashing on the airplane's wing. Soon he smelled an aroma he could recognize anywhere: "Food!"

From the odor, he couldn't tell what dinner would be. It didn't smell like chicken, it didn't smell like beef, and it certainly didn't smell like turkey. It smelled sort of like the food in his school lunchroom on a day when they were serving something awful left over from the day before.

Even when it arrived, the food was still a mystery. Everything came in one hard-to-open blue plastic box.

Once Alvin wrestled it apart, he found a cellophane packet with a napkin and a plastic fork, knife, and spoon. A second packet held salt, pepper, a pat of butter, a packet of salad dressing, and a wet napkin to clean up with when you were all through. There was also a plastic coffee cup. Underneath it all was the food, which looked as though it might have been made out of plastic itself. Alvin recognized the salad and the roll and the cake that surrounded the plate. He recognized the noodles and the broccoli. But even up close, he wasn't entirely sure what the main course was. It seemed to be a lump of something in some sort of greasy tomato sauce.

"What is this, anyhow?" Alvin asked as Dad attacked it with his knife.

"I honestly don't know," Dad said, examining the piece he had just cut. "It might be veal. Or some kind of chicken patty. We used to call this mystery meat back when I was in school."

Dad took a bite and made a face. "It's a mystery, all right."

"How does it taste?" Alvin wondered.

"Tough." Dad chewed. "But edible." Dad swallowed. "I guess."

Alvin decided to skip it for a while. He had a much better idea. He'd always wondered what it would be like to start a meal with dessert and then work his way backward to the salad. Now he had his chance.

First he took a bite of cake. "Alvin, would you mind finishing the rest of your meal before you start on dessert?" Dad requested.

"I'm trying a backwards meal," Alvin explained. "First dessert, then the main course, then the salad. Kind of dinner in reverse."

Dad just shook his head. "Suit yourself."

Alvin polished off his cake. He wolfed down the broccoli and noodles. Then he sank his knife and fork into the mysterious clump of soggy meat. Whatever it was, it tasted okay as long as he didn't use his imagination too much.

Then he picked up the little packet of salad dressing.

"Better taste that before you put it on your salad," Dad advised.

"You mean my dessert," said Alvin. "Is it awful, or what?"

"Read the label and take a guess," Dad suggested.

The label listed twenty ingredients. The only ones Alvin had heard of were vinegar, sugar, and vegetable oil, and he didn't even know how to pronounce things like xanthan gum and polysorbate-80. "Just like homemade," Dad said, "if you grew up in a chemical plant."

"I may as well try it," Alvin said. "I'll squeeze some onto my finger and have a lick."

"Alvin, we're civilized human beings. We eat with silverware, or in this case plasticware," said Dad.

"We eat bananas and hamburgers with our fingers," Alvin protested.

"Yes," Dad said. "But not soup. Or salad dressing, thank you."

Alvin tugged at the corner of the packet that said TEAR HERE. The packet didn't open.

He bit the corner and tried again. Still no luck.

Alvin tried a third time. This time the packet burst apart, squirting bright orange salad dressing all over his clean blue shirt.

Dad shook his head. "Alvin, I said we eat with silverware, not with shirts."

"It wasn't my fault, Dad. Honest." Alvin put his finger in one of the spots, picked up some dressing, and took a lick. "You're right. Yucky."

Dad wiped the messiest spots with his napkin, but a large portion of Alvin's shirt still had an orange polka-dot pattern. "Go back to the bathroom and use a wet paper towel to get those spots off before they set in," Dad said.

Alvin was in no hurry to try one of those bathrooms

36

again, but he climbed across his father and headed down the aisle. When he finally got to the back of the plane, the blue water seemed to have been mopped up, and the bathroom he'd tried had a hand-lettered OUT OF ORDER sign on it. The other door said VACANT, so Alvin went right in.

Making certain not to go anywhere near the TOILET FLUSH button, he found a paper towel, put water on it, and rubbed at the spots on his shirt. Most of them came out. Then he went back up the aisle, squeezed past a flight attendant with a stack of food trays, and found his row again.

"Alvin, how you manage to do these things is beyond me," Mom said, grabbing him by his belt.

"Come on, Mom," Alvin said, embarrassed. He had the feeling the whole plane was staring at him.

"Turn around," Mom said, inspecting his shirt.

Alvin did. "Can I please sit down now?"

"Not as bad as I'd guessed," Mom said, letting go of his belt. "Okay. Sit."

"I still say it's no fair!" Annie said. "Lambie didn't get any dinner!"

"Annie, I told you three times already," said Mom. "Lambie had dinner before we left home. He'll be just fine till we land."

"He'd better not be mad at me," Annie said. "It isn't my fault."

A voice came over the loudspeaker while Alvin was finishing his undressed-salad dessert. "This is your captain with more information about our flight. The ground temperature in Chicago is thirty-one degrees Fahrenheit, it's partly cloudy, and wind is from the west at fifteen miles per hour. We're now approaching South Bend, Indiana, so we'll be arriving at O'Hare Airport in approximately twenty minutes. That'll be around about six-thirty. You'll probably want to reset your watch if you haven't done so already. Central standard time is now six-oh-nine."

Alvin had forgotten all about the time zone change. He looked down at his watch: it said 5:09. As he fiddled with the reset buttons, Alvin realized he'd get to stay up extra late during this trip. His parents normally let him stay up later than usual on non-school nights anyhow. But whenever he had to go to bed, it would really be an hour later Sherwood Forest time.

The flight attendants took all the food trays away, and Alvin obeyed the announcement to put his seatback and tray table in the upright position and fasten his seat belt. He heard a loud clunk outside, which Dad explained was the sound of the landing gear dropping down from the wing. And he could feel the plane become quieter and slow down as it gently descended through the air.

For a while the wing lights lit up the misty clouds, and then the plane dropped into the clear air beneath them. Alvin could see lights on streets and houses and buildings below getting closer and closer.

Soon the plane was so low he could read the lettering on a bunch of fast-food restaurant signs. The next thing he knew, the plane touched down with a little thud, and the engines roared into reverse to slow it down. As the plane turned off the main runway toward the terminal, some of the passengers applauded.

Alvin joined in the applause, and so did Annie. The crew thanked everyone for flying Falcon Airways and wished everybody a happy Thanksgiving.

"Yes!" Annie shouted and began singing "Over the River and Through the Woods." Her seatmate enjoyed the performance almost as much as Alvin did.

7

"You made it!" boomed the tall gray-haired man in a "Land of Lincoln" sweatshirt and a heavy parka who just happened to be Alvin Hoople's grandfather.

"Finally!" Alvin shouted back. O'Hare Airport was so big that even after the plane landed it took nearly ten minutes to taxi to the gate. Then there was a crush of people in the aisle, and it took the Hooples a while just to make sure they weren't leaving any luggage, coats, cats, or cakes behind. Annie's seatmate wished the family a happy Thanksgiving, and the captain apologized to Alvin because there was just no time to show him the cockpit. Finally everybody had to walk down a corridor that was even longer than the one in Buffalo but didn't have a human conveyor belt or a display of Carly Cutie dolls.

Alvin's grandparents were waiting outside the security area. It reminded Alvin of his lucky quarter, which he hoped Gramps wouldn't mention. And he didn't. He just gave Alvin a hearty handshake while a skinny woman with ash-blond hair and a very wrinkly complexion hugged Mom and gave her a big kiss.

Then the woman, Alvin's grandmother, kissed and hugged him, too, right there in the middle of the airport. Alvin was slightly embarrassed, but he tried not to show it. "How was the trip?" Grandma inquired.

39

"Great!" said Alvin.

Gramps stooped down and hugged little Annie. "And how did you like your very first airplane ride?"

"I found out what the airsick bag was for!" Annie declared.

"Oh, Annie!" cried Grandma, stooping down. "Are you all right?"

"Of course," said Annie. "I didn't throw up. Not even once!"

"Well, that's because you're a big girl now!" said Grandma, giving her a hug. "If I didn't know who you were, I'd hardly recognize you!"

"See, Alvin? I am not a shrimp! And neither is Lambie!" She held the sky kennel up for Grandma and Gramps to see.

"Shrimp?" snorted Gramps. "Why, he looks almost tiger-sized to me."

"See?" Annie said, and made a face at Alvin.

Gramps stood up. "You didn't have to use the airsick bag, did you, Alvin?"

"Not me," Alvin said. "I'm planning to eat plenty of turkey tomorrow night."

"Turkey?" Gramps said as if he'd never heard the word in his life. "Grandma, did you say anything about turkey?"

Grandma frowned. "I don't think I said anything about turkey."

"Quit teasing," said Alvin. "It's Thanksgiving. You know we're going to have turkey."

Grandma and Gramps looked at each other and smiled. "I suppose it's a possibility," Grandma said.

"Well, I know we're going to have dessert, because I've got that right here." He held up the cake box.

"Alice, is that my favorite?" Gramps asked.

Mom nodded.

"What a surprise! You shouldn't have."

"Well, she did," said Grandma. "Now why don't we all get moving? Come on, everybody. Follow me!"

Talking and laughing, they rode down an escalator to the baggage-claim area. It was filled with people from the airplane crowding around a big revolving metal ring. Bags magically appeared from behind a little door and went around and around the ring until someone picked them up.

"Wow!" said Annie. "It's just like that ride in the playground, only bigger."

"It's called a carousel, too," said Gramps. "But it's only for luggage. Little girls are not allowed to go for rides on it. Or big girls, or boys, or anybody else, come to think of it."

"Too bad," said Annie. "The luggage looks like it's having fun."

Alvin had never seen so much baggage in one place. There were suitcases and duffel bags and boxes tied with twine, and there was even a long skinny box that said SKI-PAK on the side. A lot of the luggage looked just like the Hooples', but the name tags identified the real owners.

As people found their bags, the crowd thinned out. Alvin suddenly had a discouraging thought. "Do they ever lose luggage?" he asked.

Dad frowned. "On occasion."

"What if they lost ours?"

"I guess we'd have to walk around in what we have on our backs for a couple of days until they found it."

That sounded pretty smelly, but then Alvin had a worse thought. He could just see all his favorite clothes and his most important belongings disappearing forever. "What if they lost it for good?"

"I suppose the airline would pay us some money as compensation."

In that case, Alvin thought, maybe he wouldn't really mind losing his clothes and important belongings.

"And," said Gramps, "whoever found the bags might walk around for days being mistaken for the Hoople family."

"Not too likely this trip, though," said Dad. "I see one bag down there that looks awfully familiar. And there's another."

As the bags circled into reach, Dad lifted them off the carousel. Then he and Gramps carried them over to where everyone else was waiting.

"Let's go!" Annie said, picking up the sky kennel. "Lambie has to get home for dinner!"

"Not so fast!" said Gramps. "Let's button up our coats first. It's cold out there."

Annie put Lambie's carrier down again without looking. It landed right on top of the cake box.

Alvin grabbed the sky kennel. The box beneath it was smashed to half its height. "Look what you did!" Alvin scolded.

"I didn't do anything," Annie protested.

"I took care of the cake all the way from home, and you smashed it flat!"

Gramps picked up the forlorn-looking box. "Well, not quite flat. But smashed it is."

"It was so nicely decorated, too," said Mom, giving Annie a dirty look.

Gramps undid the string, lifted the lid, and looked inside. "Well, it still says 'Happy Thanksgiving.' Sort of. And there's a big black-and-white blob in the middle."

"That used to be a Pilgrim," Alvin said.

"This turned out to be a tougher journey than the *Mayflower*'s," said Mom.

Gramps stuck his finger in the box and took a lick of frosting. "Still seems to taste okay."

"Can I try some?" Alvin asked.

Gramps stuck another finger in the box and held it out to Alvin for a lick. "Excellent," Alvin declared.

"I want some, too," Annie said.

"I'm running out of fingers," Gramps protested. But somehow he found one for Annie, who managed to smear the chocolate icing all over her face.

"Enough!" said Gramps. "We'll check the rest out very carefully when we get home. Speaking of which ...let's go!" And he led the way outside, across a wide drive, and into an enormous parking lot.

One elevator ride and a long walk later, Grandma said, "Here we are!" and unlocked the back door of a van that looked like a small bus, but a lot snazzier. It was painted red, but the sides had orange flame decals. The van looked as though it were speeding through a ring of fire.

"Terrific van!" Alvin exclaimed.

Gramps smiled. "Kind of flashy, but it gets us where we're going."

"We won it in the contest," Grandma said. "It was our Early Bird bonus."

"Shhhh," Gramps said, putting his finger over his lips.

"What contest?" Alvin asked.

"Oh, never mind," said Grandma. "First things first. Let's get the luggage in so we can hit the road."

Alvin and Dad helped load the luggage in the back while everybody else climbed inside. Alvin got to ride up front with Grandma and Gramps, and Annie was none too happy about it. She insisted Lambie would get carsick if he didn't get to ride up front, but nobody seemed to hear her.

"Fasten your seat belts!" said Grandma as she backed the van out of the parking space. Three minutes later they were out of the parking lot and on the road.

"Over the river and through the woods, to Grandmother's house we go," Annie sang. This time everyone else joined in, and they all sang the entire song, including some extra lyrics Grandma and Gramps remembered. There was no doubt about it. Even if it had gotten off to a slow start, this was bound to be the best Thanksgiving ever.

8

As far as Alvin was concerned, the best thing about the ride was that Annie fell asleep a few minutes after they reached the highway and before she had a chance to pipe up with "Are we there yet?" more than once or twice. But it was too dark outside to see much. The sky was covered with thick clouds like the ones Alvin had just flown through.

What Alvin could see was that the roads were very straight, and the land was very flat, and there weren't many trees beside the road. Gramps said they were driving through the cornfields, though by now there wasn't any corn in them.

Eventually the cornfields gave way to a string of restaurants Alvin recognized from back home—all the popular hamburger, chicken, taco, and fish and chips eateries. "I wonder why nobody has a turkey restaurant," Alvin said. "You could have Thanksgiving any day of the year."

"Good idea," said Grandma. "You could call it 'Tom 'n' Trimmings'."

"Or 'Stuffin' 'n' Stuff,'" said Gramps.

"Or 'Gobble Gobble,'" said Alvin.

"It's a great idea, all right," said Gramps. "Maybe someday it'll make you a wealthy man. Speaking of which, do you still have that lucky quarter I gave you way back when?"

"That's a long story," Alvin said sheepishly.

"Well, go on," said Gramps.

Alvin explained what had happened.

"If you ask me," said Grandma, "the only thing you're missing is twenty-five cents. Lucky quarters are a silly superstition."

"I'd appreciate it, dear," said Gramps, "if you wouldn't make fun of lucky quarters that way."

"Of course you would!" Grandma said. "You carry that old quarter of yours everywhere you go!"

"I certainly wouldn't want to be without it," said Gramps. "Alvin, we'll definitely have to look into this problem."

A few minutes later Alvin saw a sign that said DOWNTOWN TYLER WISHES YOU THE BEST OF THE SEASON, and the next thing you knew, they were driving right down the little town's main street. It was all lit up for Christmas. Every shop seemed to have candles and wreaths and colored lights and Santa Clauses, and bright bells and stars above the street swayed in the breeze.

"Christmas seems to get earlier every year," Gramps grumbled. "Sooner or later they'll start celebrating on the Fourth of July."

"Christmas! Where?" Annie said, waking up instantly. She marveled at the lights and decorations and began singing "Jingle Bells." There was nothing else for anyone to do but sing along.

The van soon left the Christmas lights behind. It turned down a side street and into a broad driveway halfway up the block. Gramps made his voice high and squeaky like Annie's and shouted, "We're there yet!"

By the light from the street Alvin could see the sprawling old white house with lacy curlicues on the porch roof and tall trees in the big yard. He knew he had been there once before, years ago, but he hardly remembered it at all.

The van bounced down the driveway to a garage that was separate from the house. "Now watch this!" said Gramps.

With a great flourish, he took a remote control out of the glove compartment and aimed it at the left-hand garage door. The door opened automatically.

"We have one just like that at home," Alvin said.

"Oh, you do, do you?" said Gramps. "Can yours do this?"

He leaned back and pointed the remote control toward the house. Suddenly it blazed with light, inside and out.

"How'd you do that?" Annie exclaimed.

"It's all in this little remote control. I can even turn off the lights in just the living room. All I have to do is type in my instructions." Gramps pressed a few buttons and pointed the remote control at the house again. The lights went off in just two of the windows, but the rest stayed on.

"Can I try it?" Alvin asked.

"Can I?" asked Annie.

"Why not?" said Gramps. He showed Annie a little blue button marked REPEAT. "Now just press that blue button. Nothing else." He handed the control to her.

She pressed the button. The living room lights went off.

"What if I press it again?" she asked.

"Try it," said Gramps.

Annie did. The lights came on again. Annie giggled and pressed the button one more time. The lights went off.

"It's my turn," said Alvin.

"No!" said Annie, pressing the button again.

"Come on, Annie," Alvin said. "We want to go inside."

"We certainly do," said Mom. "Give Alvin a turn."

Annie pressed the button again. The lights went off. Annie giggled.

"You've started something you'll wish you hadn't, Dad," said Mom. Alvin always felt slightly weird when she called Gramps "Dad," even though he was her father.

"Enough, Annie," said Alvin's Dad in a stern voice.

"Phooey," said Annie, but she handed Alvin the control.

Alvin pressed the blue button a couple of times. It worked fine. There were keys with letters and numbers just like on a typewriter or computer, there were buttons from 0 to 9 just like on a push-button phone, there were a couple of tiny switches just like the ones he'd seen on the control for his friend Myron's robot, and there was a little window that showed the words LIVING ROOM LIGHTS.

"It looks like this can do just about everything," Alvin said, handing it back.

"Wait till you see!" said Gramps, putting it in his pocket. "It's absolutely astounding!"

"Expensive, too, I bet," said Dad.

"It would've been," said Gramps, getting out of the van. "But we won it."

"Won it?" Annie said.

"We'd never won anything in our lives before," Grandma explained. "This was fourth prize in one of those magazine contests."

"You mean those ones that send you letters saying 'You may have won seventeen million dollars!' and come with a whole bunch of little stickers for magazine subscriptions?" Alvin asked.

"Yup," said Gramps. "We didn't win the millions, but we did win the Electrono Home Control System. They installed it and everything, and we didn't even buy any magazines."

"Don't forget the van," said Grandma.

"Right," said Gramps. "We won that for sending our entry in early."

Alvin could hardly believe it. He'd never even met

anybody who'd ever won anything, and now his own grandparents had won two terrific prizes. "Does the remote control run a robot that'll carry our luggage to the house?" Alvin wondered.

"Nope," said Gramps. "I'm afraid we'll have to do that with good old musclepower."

A whole family's worth of good old musclepower lugged all the baggage to the back porch. "Hey, Annie!" said Gramps. "Give the doorbell a ring!"

Annie tried. "I can't reach!" she complained.

"Well, I'll just have to lift you up." Gramps set down the bags he was carrying and, with a grunt, hoisted Annie up. "Oof! You're a heavy one. Quick! Press that button before you wear me out!"

Annie pressed the button. The opening notes of Annie's holiday favorite, "Over the River and Through the Woods," wafted through the door.

Annie giggled as Gramps set her down. "Let me do that again!"

"Later," Grandma said. "First we should all go inside and get warm."

"I wholeheartedly agree," said Dad, rubbing his gloved hands together.

"Well, Alvin, open the door," said Gramps with a twinkle in his eye.

Alvin turned the doorknob. It wouldn't move. "It's locked!"

"Oh, my; I must've forgotten," Gramps said. "Do you see the keyhole?"

Alvin looked at the doorknob. There wasn't a keyhole anywhere near it. And there didn't seem to be one anywhere else in the door. "No," he said. "I don't."

Gramps handed him the remote control. "Press 2-4-5-5 and the GO button and see what happens."

Alvin pressed 2, 4, then 5 twice, and then a red button marked GO. The door swung open, a little electronic fanfare played, and an electronic-sounding voice said, "Welcome home!" Alvin was highly impressed.

"Who said that?" Annie demanded.

"It's the electronic security system," Gramps said. "Makes regular locks a thing of the past."

Dad smiled. "I guess our house in Sherwood Forest is just hopelessly out of date."

The inside of his grandparents' house was even bigger than Alvin would have guessed from the outside. And it smelled different from any place Alvin knew— kind of old-fashioned somehow. Gramps and Grandma proudly led the way through a huge kitchen and a dining room with a long wooden table and a living room with a cozy fireplace and heavy old furniture, and Alvin detoured through a bathroom full of cute little soaps and towels.

The second floor had another bathroom, along with Gramps and Grandma's bedroom and two more besides. Mom and Dad took most of the luggage into the front bedroom and began unpacking. Then Grandma and Gramps led the way up one more flight of stairs and through a door.

"This will be your bedroom, kids," said Grandma.

It didn't look like any bedroom Alvin had ever seen. The walls all sloped toward the ceiling. Fishing rods and reels hung from the walls, and above the sofa was a little trophy cup beneath a big stuffed fish.

"If this is a bedroom, where are the beds?" Annie wondered.

"You don't see any beds?" Gramps asked.

"No," said Alvin.

"Me, neither," said Annie.

"Maybe you just have to use your imagination." Gramps took the cushions off the sofa and yanked on a little handle. Then he unfolded a neatly made bed with everything but pillows.

"Where's the other one?" Annie demanded.

Gramps took the remote control from his pocket and

49

handed it to Alvin. "Press B-E-D," he said. Alvin pressed B, then E, then D. Each letter appeared in the little window.

"Now press GO," Gramps told him.

"I want to do it!" said Annie.

"It's Alvin's turn," said Grandma.

Alvin pressed the GO button. A bed slid out of the wall. "Does everything but make itself," Gramps said.

That, thought Alvin, was a shame. If there was one thing he hated, it was making his bed. He was sure people would pay big money for something that would do it automatically. But he decided this room would definitely be the most interesting place he'd ever slept.

"You two even have your very own bathroom right across the hall," Gramps pointed out. "We put Lambie's litter box in there so he can make himself at home."

"What else can you do with this remote control?" Alvin wondered.

"Well, let's see," said Gramps. "Try punching in RA-DIO."

"I want to try," said Annie.

"Annie, I'm afraid you'll have to wait till you learn to spell," said Grandma.

"I know the alphabet," said Annie.

"Annie," said Grandma, "there are some things you can't do until you're bigger."

"You said I was bigger," Annie protested.

"But you're not as big as Alvin. And I'll bet there are lots of things Alvin gets to do that you're not allowed to," Gramps said.

"Yes," said Annie. "And it's no fair, either."

Gramps picked Annie up and stared her right in the eye. "You can't do everything you want all the time, Little Miss Fussbudget. You can't drive a car, can you?"

"Neither can Alvin," said Annie as Gramps set her back onto the floor again. "And I can do anything Alvin can do. And I am not Little Miss Fussbudget, either."

Alvin had already punched in RADIO. "Now do I press GO?" he asked.

"Oh, what the heck. Let your sister do it," Gramps said. "Annie, it's the red button."

Alvin made a face. But he held the remote control where Annie could reach it. With great pride, she carefully pressed the button.

All of a sudden the room filled with music. It was classical music, the kind Alvin's father liked. Annie danced around in time to it. "How do you change the station?" Alvin wondered.

"See the little keys with the arrows?" Gramps said.

Alvin nodded.

"Press one."

Alvin did. A number appeared in the little window, and all of a sudden the music turned to loud rock that was more his style. "Is that number for the station?" he asked.

"Right again! You are one smart grandson!"

Alvin grinned.

"I'm smart, too," said Annie.

"No doubt about it," said Gramps. "Now, Alvin, if you'll just turn that loud music down a little, we'll be able to hear ourselves think."

Alvin looked at the control. He thought he might be able to use the little arrows to change the volume, but he knew they didn't work that way.

"Type in VOLUME," said Gramps, "and then hit GO."

Alvin did. "Nothing happened," he said.

"Now try the little arrows," said Gramps.

Alvin did. When he pressed the down arrow, the music got softer. The up arrow made the music louder again. "Neat!" Alvin said.

"Makes regular radios a thing of the past," Gramps said proudly. "And you can do it for any room of the house. You can have Beethoven playing in here, Duke Ellington in the kitchen, and George Prune and the

Burps in the bathroom. We've even got a second remote control so that Grandma can change her station while I adjust the microwave oven."

"I want to try," said Annie, jumping and grabbing for the remote control. But Alvin held it just out of her reach as Dad and Mom came into the room.

"Now listen here, Annie," said Mom sternly. "We don't want you fooling around with that remote control."

"But I want to," said Annie.

"Keep those little mitts off," said Dad. "You could do something very bad."

"What?" Annie demanded.

Dad looked puzzled. "What could she do?" he asked Gramps.

"Well, I suppose she could set off the burglar alarm."

"You've got a burglar alarm?" Alvin said, highly impressed.

"Comes with the system," Gramps said proudly. "Maybe later on I'll give you a demonstration."

"Great!" said Alvin. He'd never seen a burglar-alarm system before.

"I don't think it's great at all," said Annie with a pout.

"Well," said Gramps, "maybe you can be the burglar."

"Really?" said Annie.

"Absolutely," said Gramps.

Annie's gloom suddenly vanished. "I'm gonna be the burglar!" she sang. "I'm gonna be the burglar!"

"Come on, little burglar," said Grandma. "Let's go down to the kitchen. Maybe you can steal a cookie."

"I'm gonna steal *two* cookies," said Annie.

"Good for you," said Gramps with a wink.

"Then I'm gonna steal that remote control thing."

Gramps and Grandma just chuckled. But Dad and Mom gave Annie two very dirty looks.

9

The kitchen was the biggest Alvin had ever seen. It had a huge stove, a huge refrigerator, a wide counter in the middle, and cupboards everywhere. And there was a table for eating, complete with plates piled high with cookies. The little burglar stole three of them. Alvin took half a dozen himself.

"Would you like some milk?" Grandma asked.

"Sure," Alvin said.

"Help yourself," said Grandma. "It's on the door in the fridge. You can find glasses in the cupboard above the sink."

"I want some, too," said Annie.

"Alvin will get you some," said Gramps.

Alvin opened the refrigerator. It was so full of goodies some of the shelves seemed to be bending under the weight. There were jams and jellies and pickles and olives and little plastic containers full to the brim, but at the very top was the one thing Alvin had been waiting for: a giant turkey, a magnificent turkey, a turkey twice the size of the one they'd had last year. Alvin tried to imagine how big that turkey must have been when it was alive and strutting around. This was one turkey you really wouldn't want to mess with.

"So you weren't sure about the turkey!" Alvin said.

Gramps chuckled. "It's so tiny it slipped my mind."

"It's enormous!" said Alvin, setting the milk on the counter. "It's the Godzilla of turkeys!"

"I want to see!" said Annie.

"Hang on," Alvin told her. He found the glasses and filled them with milk. Then he opened the refrigerator door to put the carton back.

Annie looked inside. "That's one big turkey, all right."

"Now I'll show you something else," said Gramps. "Shut the door and press the little red button at the bottom."

"I want to do it. Let me do it!" said Annie.

Alvin pretended to press it, just to be mean. "Come on, Alvin," said Grandma. "Let your sister have a chance."

"Yes," Annie scolded. "Let your sister have a chance." With infinite care, she pressed the button.

"Refrigerator temperature, thirty-eight degrees," said a female voice from out of nowhere. "Freezer temperature, minus two degrees. Two pounds of ice available. All systems go. Have a nice day."

Annie whirled around. "Who said that?"

"The turkey," Alvin declared.

Annie yanked the refrigerator door open. "Who's in there?" she shouted. She didn't see anybody, so she tried the freezer door. "Anybody in there?"

"Haven't you heard of people talking turkey?" Alvin joked. "Well, that turkey is talking human."

"Turkeys can't talk!" Annie insisted.

"They go 'Gobble, gobble,' don't they?" asked Alvin.

"Yes, but they don't talk like people. Who's in the refrigerator?"

"Nobody's in there," said Gramps. "It's just like the security system. A little computer makes the voice. This one does sound more like a human though. Makes normal refrigerators a thing of the past."

Annie glared at her brother. "Alvin, you were teasing me again."

Alvin just smiled.

"You just wait," said Annie.

Just then Alvin's parents came through the swinging door from the dining room. "Were you teasing Annie?" Mom demanded.

But before Alvin had a chance to reply, the phone rang. "Answer it, Alvin," said Gramps.

Alvin looked around. He didn't see a phone anywhere. "Where is it?" he asked.

"In the turkey," Gramps said. "It's a drumstickophone."

"Come on," said Alvin.

Gramps handed him the remote control. "Press the PHONE button."

Alvin pressed the button. "Hello!" Gramps shouted.

"Hello?" said a woman's voice that filled the room from nowhere that Alvin could see.

"Hi, Irene!" said Grandma in a normal tone of voice. "Where are you?"

"We're in the motel. We got here just fine."

"Who is that?" Annie asked.

"It's your Aunt Irene," Mom said softly. "Marty's mom. Hi, Irene!"

"Hi, Alice!" said the voice.

"Where is she?" Annie demanded.

"Good question," said Gramps. "Where are you, Irene?"

"Not quite two hundred miles from you," said Aunt Irene. "We'll get an early start tomorrow. Should be there before lunch. How was the trip, Alice?"

"We had a wonderful flight," said Mom.

"Was that Annie I heard before?"

"Yes!" Annie cried. "I didn't even get carsick!"

"Well, we'll see you tomorrow," said the voice. "Marty says hello to Alvin."

"Hello back," said Alvin, though he wasn't all that crazy about seeing Marty.

"Drive carefully," said Grandma.

55

"We certainly will. Good night!"

"Good night!" said Gramps.

"Speaking of which," said Dad, "I believe it's somebody's bedtime." And he stared right at Annie and Alvin.

"Since when do I have to go to bed the same time as Annie?" Alvin demanded.

"It's past both your bedtimes," said Dad. "It's even later if you figure it on Sherwood Forest time."

"It's not my bedtime yet," Annie shrieked. "I have to be the burglar!"

"You were exactly the same way when you were young, Alice," said Grandma with a smile. "You didn't want to go to bed, either."

"See?" Alvin said.

"As I recall," said Mom to her mom, "you made me go whether I wanted to or not."

"Uh-oh," said Annie.

"Annie, you may play the burglar first thing in the morning," said Gramps. "Right now you're going to play Sleeping Beauty."

"That's what you think," said Annie.

"Funny. That's what I think, too," said Dad. And he picked her up and whisked her away before she could even say good night.

10

While Dad put Annie and Lambie to bed, Mom and Alvin rooted around in the suitcases and found his pajamas, his slippers, and his bathrobe. Gramps gave him a towel, toothpaste, dental floss, and his own personal sanitary bristles for the electric toothbrush.

Alvin tiptoed upstairs to the bathroom and put on his pajamas. The electric toothbrush spattered toothpaste all over the mirror and his bathrobe the first time he tried it, but he cleaned things up and got the hang of it the second time. Then, careful not to wake Annie, he crept across the hall to the bedroom and crawled into the sofa bed.

"Is that you, Alvin?" said someone who sounded suspiciously like his little sister.

"Be quiet," said Alvin. "You're supposed to be asleep."

"Well, I'm not!" said Annie. "And neither is Lambie."

"You'd both better go to sleep right now," said Alvin. "You know it's way past your bedtime."

"I can't sleep. It's too dark in here."

"It's not too dark. There's a night-light right over there."

"It doesn't have a funny red nose like my clown one at home."

"Maybe not, but it's just as bright. Now go to sleep." Actually, Alvin was as excited and wide awake as his little sister, but he enjoyed telling her what to do.

"I told you, it's too dark," Annie complained. "It's spooky. There are creepy shadows all over the place. That big fish on the wall might fall down and bite me."

Alvin looked around. He had to admit if you had Annie's kind of imagination, the shadows probably would look pretty creepy. And the fish's sharp teeth did look fierce. "How about if I turn on the light in the hallway?"

"Maybe," said Annie.

Alvin went out the door and turned on the hall light. On his way back, he left the bedroom door partway open. "Now, how's that?"

"Too bright," said Annie.

Alvin closed the door until it was open just a crack. "It's fine now," he said, climbing into bed again. "Go to sleep. Good night."

"I want a drink of water."

"There are paper cups in the bathroom," said Alvin.

"I can't reach them. I want *you* to bring me a drink," said Annie.

Alvin was beginning to see why his parents always seemed to make faces at each other when they said, "Isn't it Annie's bedtime?"

"If I bring it to you, will you shut up and go to sleep?" he asked.

"Yes," said Annie.

Alvin found his slippers and clomped across the hall to the bathroom. On the way back, he tried to remember how his parents handled it when he was little and tried to pull the same bedtime stunts.

"Sit up," he said, handing the little cup to Annie. "Don't spill it."

Annie sat up, took the cup, and drank it down in one gulp. "More," she said, handing it back.

"This is positively the last one," Alvin said as he

headed back to the bathroom. But it took two more after that to quench Annie's sudden thirst. "Thank you," she said finally.

"You're welcome," he said. "Nighty-night."

"Nighty-night," said Annie. And she didn't say another thing for at least seventeen seconds.

Then she announced that she had to go to the bathroom.

"I can't do that for you," Alvin said.

"I know that, silly. Where are my slippers?"

"I didn't steal them."

"Yes, you did. I had my fuzzy blue bunny slippers right here, and now they're gone."

"Then go to the bathroom without them."

"I can't. The floor is too cold. And I don't want to get my feet all dirty."

"If I find your slippers, will you go to the bathroom and then go to sleep?"

"Yes."

Alvin put on his slippers, turned on the lights, and wondered what would happen if he used the remote control to slide the bed into the wall while Annie was still in it.

"See?" she said. "They're gone."

Alvin looked under her bed. The glass eye of one fuzzy blue bunny stared back at him. "Here's one," he said, reaching under and pulling it out.

"But where's the other one?" Annie demanded.

Alvin looked around the room again. There was no other bunny anywhere on the floor. Then he noticed one fuzzy blue ear sticking up from the covers at the bottom of Annie's bed. He picked up the slipper and handed it to her.

Annie carefully put each slipper on. Then she discovered she had put them on wrong. She switched them around and went to the bathroom. By the time she came back and got into her bed, Alvin was almost asleep himself.

"Alvin, this pillow smells funny."

"It does not smell funny!" Alvin shouted in exasperation. "It smells fine! Will you go to sleep?"

"How do you know?"

"I just know."

"Did you smell it?"

"No."

"Well, come here and smell for yourself. It smells funny."

"Annie, go to sleep!"

"I won't unless you come here and sniff this pillow."

"All right!" Alvin went over to Annie's bed. She was already holding out the pillow.

Alvin sniffed it. "Smells okay to me."

"You didn't sniff the right place. Sniff *there*." She poked her finger right in the middle.

It still smelled okay to Alvin. "Annie, there is nothing wrong with this pillow."

"Are you sure?"

"Yes."

"Are you positive?"

"Yes."

"Well, okay, then." She fluffed it up and lay her head back down on it.

By now Alvin was sure he wasn't going to get to sleep. He was positive Annie would have just one more request.

And she did. "Alvin, tell me a story."

"No! You promised you'd go to sleep."

"I will if you tell me a story. A bedtime story."

"I'll tell you a story, all right."

"Good."

"Okay. You listening?"

"Yes."

"Once upon a time—"

"I like bedtime stories," said Annie.

"Be quiet and listen," said Alvin. "Once upon a time

there was a little girl named Annie who refused to go to sleep."

"I don't want to hear this story," Annie says. "Daddy tells this one all the time."

Alvin wasn't the least bit surprised. "This story only starts the same way. It's not the same story."

"It better not be," said Annie.

"Okay. Once upon a time, this little girl named Annie refused to go to sleep. First she wanted a glass of water. Then she wanted to go to the bathroom. Then she couldn't find her slippers. Then she thought her pillow smelled funny. And then she made somebody tell her a bedtime story just like this."

"You're a liar. This is *just* like the one Daddy tells."

"Just wait," said Alvin. "She was listening to the story, when all of a sudden she heard this very mysterious sound."

"What kind of very mysterious sound?"

Alvin tried to think of a mysterious sound that would put his sister to sleep. Suddenly the lights came on, and he heard a *Whoop! Whoop!* noise like the ones police cars made in Sherwood Forest. A weird electronic voice began gurgling "Burglar alert! Burglar alert!" in time with the whooping.

"Wow!" Annie cried. "Then what happened?"

11

The whoop-whooping and the "Burglar alert!" seemed to get louder and louder. "That's a mysterious noise, all right," said Annie.

"Annie, that's not part of the story," Alvin said. "That's for real."

"It is?" Annie cried. "Then where's Lambie?" She jumped out of bed without even bothering to put on her bunny slippers.

"Stay there!" said Alvin.

"No!" Annie cried. "I need to find Lambie."

"Come back here, Annie!" Alvin warned. "If there are burglars, it might be dangerous."

"I don't care. I won't let those burglars take my Lambie!"

Alvin put on his slippers and followed her down the stairs. All the lights were on in every room in the house. Grandma, Annie, and Alvin's parents, all in their pajamas, stood at the top of the stairs that led down to the living room. Down at the bottom, Gramps was pointing his remote control every which way.

"Seems to be a false alarm," he declared.

"Of course it is!" said Grandma. "Who'd want to break in here? What would anybody want to steal?"

Dad grinned. "Maybe that expensive alarm contraption."

Gramps gave the remote control a puzzled look as he came back upstairs. "Well, folks, now you've had a demonstration of the burglar alarm."

"But there aren't any burglars," said Alvin, slightly disappointed.

"Well, nobody said the system was one hundred percent perfect," said Gramps.

"The only thing that's being stolen around here is our sleep," said Mom wearily. "Back to bed, everybody."

"But I don't want the burglars to get Lambie," said Annie.

"Didn't you hear?" Alvin said. "There aren't any burglars."

"If there aren't any burglars, where's Lambie?" Annie demanded.

"He's not upstairs with you?" Mom asked.

"No! The burglars took him!" Annie shrieked.

"You know what?" said Dad. "I'll bet that cat is our culprit."

Gramps slapped himself on the forehead. "Of course! He probably snuck downstairs and ran past the motion detectors."

"We'd better find him," said Dad. "Unless we put him upstairs for keeps, the same thing is bound to happen again."

So everyone hunted high and low. Ten minutes later, Grandma found Lambie fast asleep behind the big grandfather clock in the living room. A very relieved Annie carried him upstairs.

"Now keep this closed tight," Dad said, showing Alvin a door at the top of the stairs. "We do not want to be burglarized again by that cat."

"Good night, once and for all," said Mom.

Annie and Lambie snuggled together, and Alvin lay his head down on the pillow.

"Tell me the rest of my story," Annie demanded.

"Annie, go to sleep."

"But I want to find out about the noise."

"You're the only noise around here. Go to sleep."

"Please, Alvin."

"Oh, all right." He tried to remember where he had left off.

"There was a very mysterious sound," Annie said.

"Oh, yeah. Okay. There was a very mysterious sound. The girl wondered what it was. She got up and went to the door, and she opened it. But nobody was there."

"Uh-oh," said Annie.

"So she went to the window and took a look outside. But nobody was there, either."

"Then what happened?"

Alvin thought hard. He liked the idea of having a giant turkey with a bloody neck sneak in from the closet, but he thought that might give Annie nightmares and keep her awake all night. He decided to stall. "Then the little girl heard a different mysterious sound."

"What?"

"It was more of a 'gobble, gobble.' The other sound was kind of a cackle."

"What did she do then?"

"She went to the window again. She went to the door again. But nobody was there."

"Then what happened?"

Alvin still hadn't figured that out yet. "Then she heard a third sound. And it was different from the first two."

"What did it sound like?"

"It sounded more like 'munch, munch.'"

"I know, I know. She went to the window and she went to the door. But nobody was there."

"Right," said Alvin. "Then she heard all three mysterious sounds at once."

64

"And she went to the window and went to the door, but nobody was there, right?"

"No," said Alvin. "She went to sleep. And she didn't hear the sounds anymore, and whatever they were went away."

"Alvin, that's the dumbest story I ever heard. That's not even the end."

"Maybe not, but it's time for you to go to sleep."

"I want to hear the end of the story."

"If you go to sleep right now, maybe I'll tell you the end tomorrow night."

"I want to hear it now."

Dad stuck his head in the door. "I thought I heard noises in here. Are you two still up?"

Annie giggled. Alvin didn't say a word.

"Because if you are, you may find yourself sleeping right through turkey tomorrow. Now get to sleep right this minute!"

Dad shut the door again. Alvin lay his head on his pillow and closed his eyes. Annie whispered, "I want to hear what happened."

"Tomorrow," Alvin whispered back. "Now go to sleep."

Whoop! Whoop! Whoop! "Burglar alert! Burglar alert!" All the lights went on again.

"Is Lambie with you?" Alvin asked, but he was sure he knew the answer.

"The burglars got him for real!" Annie shrieked.

But Alvin knew what had happened, even before Dad came up the stairs with Lambie in his arms. "This guy just won't stay put!" said Dad. "He must have crept out when I opened the door to talk to you. Now, good night for the very last time."

"You are very bad," Annie told Lambie. And she drifted right off to sleep.

But Alvin lay awake in bed. The story without an ending had made him anything but sleepy. He tried thinking about an ending, but scary monsters were all he could think of, and they kept him wide awake. He tried lying on his back, his side, and his stomach. Finally he decided to get a glass of water.

As he tiptoed back from the bathroom, he thought he noticed a flash of light in the crack between the curtains. He went to the window and drew them apart.

The first snowflake of the season fluttered down before his eyes. Another one followed it. Then another. Suddenly dozens of snowflakes filled the air. Then hundreds. Then thousands. It was magical.

Alvin left the curtains open, lay back in bed, and counted snowflakes. Five minutes later he was dreaming of giant snowmen—and snow turkeys.

12

Lambie woke up first on Thanksgiving morning. Alvin was next, because the first thing Lambie did was jump up beside Alvin's head, lie down beside him, and purr hard in his ear.

Alvin looked around. Annie was still asleep. And there was frost all over the window. Alvin put on his bathrobe and scraped a little hole in the thin film of ice.

Everything outside was white. Big wet snowflakes were falling heavily from the sky, and tree branches drooped under the weight of the snow that had already fallen. The sky was white, the roofs were white, and the wind sent white swirls skittering across the big white yard.

It felt like Christmas. Alvin could almost imagine going downstairs and finding presents under a huge tree. But Thanksgiving was a presentless holiday, and there was nothing he could do about it.

Still, Thanksgiving was a food-filled holiday, and wonderful smells were already rising into the room. Alvin went downstairs to investigate. He walked into the dining room and through the swinging door to the kitchen, and there he found Grandma and Gramps hunched over the stove. The giant turkey was on the counter beside them, and over the hidden loudspeakers came soft, old-fashioned tunes Alvin had never heard before.

"Well, good morning," said Gramps.

"How'd you sleep?" asked Grandma.

"Fine," Alvin said, peeking into Gramps's frying pan. "Wow! Sausages and home fries! My favorites!"

Gramps was every bit as good a cook as Grandma, and his sausages and home fried potatoes were famous far and wide. The local paper had even printed a picture of him fixing his special recipe for a big block party.

"Can't keep a secret from you when it comes to food," Gramps said.

Alvin stuck his nose toward the pan. "Smells great!"

"Changed your mind about eggs?" Gramps asked, pointing to some scrambled eggs he was fixing on the stove.

Alvin made a face. "Nope."

"If you don't like them this way, I can make hard-boiled, soft-boiled, poached, fried, or omelets," Gramps offered.

Alvin shuddered. "I don't like them any way. I don't like the way they look, I don't like the way they smell, and I don't like the way they taste. The only thing I hate even more is liver."

"A nice slice of liver and onions? Now, that's good eating!" said Gramps.

Alvin made a face.

"Your mother didn't like eggs when she was your age, either," Grandma said. "Now she loves them."

"I guess she must have got dumber when she grew up," said Alvin.

"You wait and see," said Gramps. "You'll change your tune."

"I won't change it to 'I Am the Egg Man,' that's for sure."

"How about 'I'm a Liver Lover'?" Gramps asked.

Alvin made a face. Then he looked in Grandma's pan. "Is that for breakfast, too?"

"That happens to be the stuffing," Grandma informed him.

"It doesn't look much like stuffing."

"Not yet," Grandma agreed. "So far, it's only onions and celery. But just you wait."

"You don't have any objections to stuffing, do you?" Gramps asked.

"Quit kidding," said Alvin. "You know Grandma's stuffing is one of my favorite things in the whole world. I just hope you're making enough."

"There'll be enough, all right. That turkey's a twenty-five-pounder, and it's got plenty of room inside," said Grandma.

"What time will it be ready?"

"How does dinnertime sound?" asked Gramps.

"You know what I mean."

"About six o'clock," said Grandma. "Think you can hold out that long?"

"Some of those sausages and home fries should help," Alvin said.

Gramps poked one of the sausages with a fork. "Another couple of minutes yet. How about some juice?"

"Sure!" said Alvin.

Grandma tossed him half a dozen oranges, one at a time. "What am I supposed to do with these?" he wondered.

"Give 'em a squeeze!" she said.

Alvin squeezed one like a tennis ball, but he knew that wasn't what Grandma had in mind. She showed him where to put them in the top of a fancy electric juicer. Then she showed him which button to press, and orange juice flowed into a little plastic pitcher. "Just another of the things we won," Grandma said proudly.

Gramps went to the window and looked out. "Quite an accumulation out there," said Gramps. "And there's

70

more on the way. It's supposed to fall all day. A real old-fashioned blizzard. I just hope your aunt and cousin can get through."

"Wow!" said Alvin, filling three glasses with juice. "Maybe we'll get snowed in!" The idea of having to stay at his grandparents' house a few extra days sounded okay to him.

Gramps flipped the home fries in the pan. "Not much chance of that," he said. "Look at the sidewalks."

Alvin looked out the window. Even though everything else had a deep coating of snow, the sidewalks were still clear. So was the driveway. "The snow's not sticking," Alvin said.

"Right you are," Gramps replied. "And do you know why not?"

Alvin thought for a minute. "Electric sidewalks!"

"Precisely, my intelligent grandson. They're electrically heated. Snow shovels are a thing of the past!"

In some ways, this was the best invention yet. Shoveling sidewalks had never been one of Alvin's favorite activities, particularly when it cut into time that could be spent sledding or just fooling around in the snow.

"How about some breakfast?" Gramps asked.

He didn't have to ask twice. Breakfast was great. The fresh-squeezed orange juice tasted as though it had just come from the tree. Gramps's home fried potatoes were even crispier than usual, and the sausage was as hot and spicy as Alvin remembered it.

But the conversation was best of all. Alvin's grandparents wanted to hear all about Alvin's Halloween, and Alvin was glad to oblige. They seemed particularly pleased to hear that Alvin was doing well in school, and they were very interested in hearing what he wanted for Christmas.

Alvin decided that the great thing about his grandparents was that they really listened to him. Sometimes when he told his parents about something like the presents he wanted, they would kind of tune out

71

and say they'd see and mention something about Alvin being good for the rest of the year. But when he told Grandma and Gramps about the bicycle he had his heart set on, they paid close attention and asked a lot of questions and even told him about the weird bikes without gears or hand brakes that they had when they were kids.

Alvin took second helpings of everything on his plate. "Just save room for the turkey," Grandma said.

"There's always room for turkey," said Alvin.

"I know exactly what you mean," said Gramps.

Alvin was just finishing his meal when a pair of fuzzy blue bunnies padded into the room.

"Good morning, Mary Sunshine," said Grandma.

"I'm not Mary Sunshine," said Annie. "I'm Ann L. Hoople."

Grandma put her hand to her brow. "How could I have forgotten!"

Alvin decided this was an excellent time to get dressed. Having breakfast with Annie was one thrill he could do without.

As he used the electric toothbrush, Alvin thought about all the neat things he could do in the snow. Then he realized all his clean clothes were in the suitcases in his parents' bedroom.

He put on his bathrobe and went back downstairs. The door to the bedroom was closed. He wanted to wake his parents up, but he knew that wouldn't be such a hot idea. Still, maybe they were up already. Alvin put his ear to the door. The only sound he heard was his father's snoring.

Back in the kitchen, Grandma and Gramps were praising Annie for her wonderful rendition of the alphabet song. They encouraged her to sing it again. Annie was glad to oblige.

"I've got a problem," Alvin broke in.

"Now I have to start all over again," said Annie, upset at being interrupted right at S.

Alvin ignored her. "All my clothes are in Mom and Dad's room."

"How about what you wore yesterday?" Grandma asked.

"I don't think they'd want me playing in the snow in those. And I'm not sure if we even packed my galoshes."

"Well, I don't think they'd be terribly happy if you woke them up," said Gramps. "You'd better wait."

"I wonder why they're so tired, anyway."

"I suspect it may have something to do with being a parent," said Gramps.

"You're Mom's parent," Alvin pointed out, "and you're not fast asleep."

"When you get to be your mom's age, your mom won't be fast asleep, either." Grandma laughed. "You'll figure it out someday."

"Why don't you watch the Thanksgiving Day parades till your folks wake up?" Gramps suggested.

"Parades!" cried Annie. "I love parades!"

Between the snow and the food, Alvin had forgotten all about the Thanksgiving Day parades on TV. And even though he was beginning to suspect he was too old for them, they were a once-a-year event, and he didn't really want to miss them. So he followed Gramps and Annie into the den.

The den was right next to the kitchen. It had wood-paneled walls covered with posters for old movies, but the only one Alvin had ever heard of was *King Kong*. Two fish, even bigger than the ones in the bedroom, hung from the ceiling. And at the far end was the biggest TV screen Alvin had ever seen. It was nearly as tall as he was. In fact, it was more like a movie screen than a TV.

Gramps showed Alvin how to use the remote control to change the channels. There were parades on three channels, and if you knew how, you could put one channel at the top of the screen and the other two in little corners at the bottom. The only one you could hear was the one at the top, but you could use the remote control to choose which channel would appear there. Switching things around meant pressing a bunch of buttons, but Alvin got the hang of it pretty fast.

Letting her brother do it was not Annie's idea of a good time. "I want to try!" she shouted.

"Didn't we have this discussion before?" Gramps said with a twinkle in his eye.

"Huh?" Annie said.

Gramps took Alvin aside. "You'll have to let her use the control a little bit."

"But that's silly. She doesn't know how!"

"You'll have to help her. You set everything up. Then let her press the GO button."

"I want to use that thing!" Annie cried.

"See what I mean?" Gramps whispered to Alvin. Then he stooped down to Annie. "Okay, Annie. Alvin's going to let you give it a try. But the only button I want you to push is this one." He pointed to the red button marked GO. "Okay?"

"But I want to know what the other buttons do."

"Alvin will show you. But don't you press anything but that red one. Okay?"

"Okay," said Annie.

"Enjoy yourselves," said Gramps, and left the room.

"I want to try!" Annie cried the instant Gramps had disappeared.

Alvin held it out of her reach. "You heard what Gramps said. Don't press anything but the red one."

"Okay," Annie said.

Alvin handed her the remote control. She pressed the red GO button, and two of the pictures traded places on the screen. "I want to try again," said she.

"Just one more time," said Alvin.

Annie pressed the button. "Nothing happened."

"Nothing was supposed to happen," said Alvin.

"But I want something to happen."

"Later. Pipe down and watch the parade."

Annie piped down and turned toward the screen, where floats and balloons and bands and majorettes were marching along. Not-so-famous television stars described the action as though nothing so important, astonishing, and amazing had ever taken place in the history of the universe.

Then came some singers. "Hey, they're not really singing!" Annie cried. "They're just moving their mouths!"

"That's for sure," said Alvin. The singers were so phony, so obvious about mouthing the words to something they'd recorded long before, that even a two-year-old would have noticed. It wasn't even in sync. "Look at that guy. Words are coming out of his mouth when it's closed. Next thing you know the balloons will start singing."

The big helium-filled balloons of cartoon characters didn't sing, which was probably just as well. But the commercial jingles more than made up for them. There were ads for candy and cereals like the ones on the weekend-morning shows. But mostly there were toy commercials.

It seemed to Alvin that three minutes couldn't go by without a bunch of commercials for a bunch of new toys or new accessories for old toys. Even with the remote control, he couldn't change channels to avoid them, because all three stations ran their commercials at the same time. There were commercials for dolls, there were commercials for toy cars, there were commercials for robots, and there were commercials for games. And Annie claimed she wanted every single thing she saw.

"You don't want a dump truck that can run over other dump trucks," said Alvin.

"Yes, I do," said Annie.

"You don't want a stuffed pig that comes with its own birth certificate," said Alvin.

"Yes, I do," said Annie.

It didn't matter what it was: Annie said she wanted it, and that was that. Alvin remembered when he was Annie's age and wanted everything, too. He wondered how his parents could have stood it.

"That's what I want most of all!" Annie cried, pointing to one of the little pictures in the corner of the screen. "Change the channel!"

"Don't be silly, Annie."

"Change it!" she shrieked in a voice so loud it made Gramps stick his nose in the door and say, "Simmer down in there."

Alvin changed the channel, but he knew what he was going to hear. The one toy Annie wanted most in the whole world next to a Carly Cutie doll was a FuzzBot. It was a giant stuffed robot that could turn into half a dozen different kinds of furry animals. Alvin thought it was the stupidest toy he'd ever seen. And by now he knew the jingle by heart, since Annie had heard it on all the Saturday-morning cartoon shows for weeks and sang it almost every chance she got.

> FuzzBots are tough with a hide of fur,
> FuzzBots are fun for him and her.
> FuzzBots can be anything you please,
> FuzzBots are lots of fun to squeeze.
> FuzzBots are cute,
> FuzzBots are hot,
> So get yourself
> Your own FuzzBot.

"FuzzBots by ToyBotics," said the announcer. "Clothes and accessories sold separately."

"That's my favorite toy in the whole world," said Annie.

"That's the dumbest toy in the whole world," said Alvin. "Who ever heard of a fuzzy robot? It's just stupid, that's all."

"It certainly is," said a silly voice at the door.

"Is not," said Annie.

She and Alvin turned toward the voice. It was coming from a tall grown-up in a curly green wig, a big plastic nose, a bushy fake moustache and eyebrows, and glasses with windshield wipers on them. There was snow all over this person's fur coat. "It is too stupid," the comical figure said, "and I should know."

Alvin remembered who it must be. "Uncle Walt!" Uncle Walt was his mother's older brother, and at family gatherings he was always the comedian and prankster. He had a million jokes and gags and card tricks—most of them really silly.

Uncle Walt came over to Alvin and extended his hand. "Murgatroyd! Long time no see!" As they shook hands, the windshield wipers on the glasses started working. "Awfully snowy out there. Good thing I brought these along."

Uncle Walt went over to Annie. "And you must be little Noodlehead."

Even Annie had to giggle. "No, I'm not."

"Not little Noodlehead? Who are you, then?"

"I'm Annie!"

"Annie! You can't be Annie! Annie's a little teeny tiny girl who can barely talk!"

"But I am! I'm Annie!"

"You look just like Noodlehead to me!"

"Well, I'm not. Alvin, who is this person?"

"Don't you remember Uncle Walt?" Alvin said. "He's Mom's brother."

"Murgatroyd doesn't know what he's talking about," said Uncle Walt. "I'm Hairy McDonut."

"You are not," said Annie.

Uncle Walt whipped off his disguise. "All right, you win. How did you ever guess?"

"I just knew!" Annie said.

"Okay. You two look bigger than last time I saw you, so I'll skip that part and let you watch the parades. Seen any good Christmas toys?"

"About two dozen, if you believe Annie," said Alvin.
"Where is everybody?"

"Grandma and Gramps were in the kitchen last I looked," Alvin said. "I'm not sure Dad and Mom are even up yet."

"Well, this outfit ought to wake anybody up. Let me put this stuff on again."

He put on his false nose, then his eyeglasses, moustache, eyebrows, and wig. "How do I look?"

"Really stupid," Alvin said.

"Terrific!" said Uncle Walt. "See you guys later."

"That guy sure is silly," Annie said.

"That's for sure!"

"Wait a minute! Change the channel, Alvin! Quick!"

Alvin looked up and saw what Annie was talking about. A Carly Cutie commercial was starting in one of the little pictures at the bottom of the screen. It was one commercial too many for Alvin. He changed the channel, made sure he had the remote control with him, and decided to go see if Uncle Walt had any more tricks up his sleeve.

But before he could get up, he heard someone else say, "Is that the dumbest song you've ever heard, or what?"

Alvin turned toward the doorway. Standing there was a plump hulk about his height and covered in snow from stocking cap to toe.

"It's Frosty the Snowman!" Annie squealed.

13

"No, it isn't," said Alvin. "It's Cousin Marty."

"It's really coming down out there," Marty said as he stood in the doorway and dripped. "We skidded off the road twice, and a truck nearly rammed into us. Then I tripped and fell in the snow outside. It's lucky we're here at all."

Alvin wondered if *lucky* was the word he'd use to describe it. He'd had a pretty good time staying at Marty's house in Philadelphia last summer, but there were times when Marty could be a big fat pain.

"Hey! Nice TV!" Marty said. "Too bad all that's on right now is all that junk for little kids."

"Marty, will you come here and help with the luggage?" said a short, stout woman who stuck her head in the door.

"In a minute," said Marty. In one graceful motion, he grabbed a piece of candy from a dish, unwrapped it, and popped it into his mouth.

"Hi, Aunt Irene," said Alvin.

"Hi, Alvin. And how are you, Annie?"

"Shhh. I'm watching Bullwinkle," Annie said as the helium-filled moose floated along the TV screen.

"Excuse me!" said Marty's mom. "Come on, Marty. Let's boogie. It'll only take a second."

"Oh, all right," Marty grumped. He followed her out the door.

Alvin and Annie watched half a dozen more commercials. Annie wanted everything, of course, but this time she paid particular attention to the Carly Cutie doll. When she sang along with the jingle, Alvin decided he'd positively had his fill of parades.

"Is there anything else to eat around here?" Marty asked, making another assault on the candy dish as he came through the door. "I'm starving."

"There's a whole refrigerator full of food," Alvin said. "Grandma said to help ourselves. Just don't eat anything that's for dinner."

"How am I supposed to know what's for dinner and what's not?"

"You can bet the turkey's for dinner. And the cranberry sauce and the stuffing." Alvin was beginning to get hungry just mentioning them. He followed Marty out to the kitchen.

"Now, this is what I call a refrigerator," Marty said, rummaging around with the instincts of a professional. In no time at all, he found bread, cheese, lunchmeat, lettuce, and mustard, and turned them into a big sandwich. "Want one?" he asked with his mouth full.

Alvin thought about it. He could have eaten something, but he didn't want to spoil his supper. "I don't know," he said finally. "I had a big breakfast."

"Did Gramps fix one of his specials again?"

"Yeah. With sausage and home fried potatoes and everything."

"I had a couple of big waffles and some bacon and eggs and home fries at the motel. It was all right, but nobody beats Grandma and Gramps when it comes to cooking." Marty took another bite of his sandwich. "Sure you don't want one?"

It did look good. "Maybe half of one," Alvin said.

"Alvin, come quick!" cried Annie from the den.

"What's the matter?" he shouted, wondering what

kind of trouble his little sister could get into in such a hurry.

"Come here! Hurry!"

Alvin strode into the den. Annie was pointing to the little picture in the bottom of the screen. "It's Santa Claus!"

"Oh, it is not," said Marty.

"It is too," cried Annie. "Make him bigger, Alvin! Quick!"

Alvin pressed a couple of buttons on the remote control and Santa sprang to life on the top part of the screen. A marching band played "Santa Claus Is Coming to Town."

"Give me a break!" said Marty. "Santa Claus!"

"It is! It's Santa Claus!" said Annie.

"Of course that isn't Santa Claus, dimwit," said Marty. "Santa Claus only comes at Christmas."

"I know what Santa Claus looks like, and that's him!" Annie insisted.

"Then who's that?" Marty demanded. He pointed to the bottom right corner of the screen. A different Santa Claus in a different parade in a different city was riding in a different float.

"That's Santa Claus, too!" said Annie.

"They're two different parades, in two different cities," Marty pointed out. "How can Santa Claus be two places at the same time?" Marty said.

Annie sucked her thumb.

"Marty, why don't you shut up?" said Alvin.

"Maybe the next float will have the tooth fairy," Marty snorted. "She has to learn the truth sometime."

"Not right before Christmas, in the middle of the Thanksgiving Day parades."

"I remember now," said Annie. "Those aren't really Santas. They're Santa's helpers. They work in the North Pole all year, but at Christmastime they go all around to help him."

"Where's Santa, then?" Marty demanded.

81

"Santa is at the department store in the mall, smarty pants," said Annie firmly. "I'm going to see him in person tomorrow and tell him what I want for Christmas. Grandma told me so."

Marty slapped his head. "Boy, I'm glad I don't have to put up with a little sister," he said. "What a dope!"

"You're the dope!" Annie said, and Alvin was tempted to agree with her. But before he got the chance, Uncle Walt came through the door shouting, "Anybody interested in lunch?"

Marty was out the door in a flash.

14

Alvin didn't want to spoil his appetite for turkey, so he tried not to eat too much at lunch. He had only one helping of homemade lasagna, a couple of handfuls of potato chips, a bunch of cookies, a glass of milk, and a hunk of what Gramps called Heavenly Smash cake. Annie picked at her food and called the lasagna "slimy stuff," but Marty didn't agree. He had seconds of everything, and thirds of the cake.

Afterward, Gramps and Dad went into the den to watch football on TV. Grandma was almost as big a football fan as Alvin's Dad, so she brought a little portable TV into the kitchen so she and Gramps wouldn't have to miss any of the game when they had to attend to the turkey. Alvin's mom and Uncle Walt and Aunt Irene stayed in the living room and talked about the old days when they all lived in the house together. And Alvin went upstairs to get dressed.

Alvin wasn't a football fan, and Marty refused to watch any team except the Philadelphia Eagles, and they both felt like outsiders listening to their parents reminisce about old times. Marty suggested playing cards, but Alvin couldn't imagine staying inside when there was all that great snow coming down and blowing around outside.

"Do you have any sleds?" he asked his grandparents in the den.

"Seems to me we ought to have a couple of real old ones around someplace," said Gramps.

"Maybe out in the garage," said Grandma. "Or down in the basement."

"I'll help you look if you like, Alvin," said Gramps, "but it's getting too deep out there for sleds anyhow. The snow will already be over the runners."

"Besides," said Dad without taking his eyes off the game, "the country around here is flat as a pancake. There aren't any hills, so you can't go belly flopping the way you do back home. Hey! Look at that pass!"

Alvin thought it over. What was the use of a sled if you couldn't go whooshing down a hill flat on your stomach?

"Do you want to go look?" Gramps asked.

"Maybe later," Alvin said. "I think we'll go out and fool around for a while first."

Alvin and Marty bundled up, borrowed some boots from Gramps, and went out the front door. The wind blew fresh snow right in their faces. It was already up to the very tops of Alvin's big, floppy galoshes—a little too high for sledding, even if there had been hills. But it was perfect snowball snow, heavy and wet and sticky. Alvin and Marty made a couple of snowballs and aimed them at the nearest telephone pole. They both came close.

Then a perfect target came out the door looking exactly like a little pink elf. Marty couldn't resist lobbing a snowball at Annie.

"Nyaah, nyaah," she shouted. "You missed!"

"I won't this time," said Marty, running toward her as he packed a clump of snow between his gloves.

"Hey, Marty, she's too little!" said Alvin. "Cut it out!"

Marty whirled and threw his snowball at Alvin. Alvin threw one back. They both missed.

84

"Stop it, you two," Annie shouted. "I want to make a snowman like Frosty in the song."

"Go ahead," said Alvin.

"Help me!" Annie cried.

"We're not going to make a snowman. We're going to build snow forts."

"Right," said Marty. "Then we can have a real snowball battle. Snowmen are for little kids."

"Well, I'm a little kid, and I'm going to make Frosty," said Annie.

"Suit yourself," Alvin shouted.

So while Alvin and Marty rolled big snowballs for their snow fort, Annie kept gathering snow into her little hands and squooshing it together. At first it was fun. Then she noticed something. "Hey, Alvin, how do you make a snowman, anyhow?"

"Do what we're doing," Alvin called as he rolled a growing snowball along the ground. "Make a snowball, then roll it and make it bigger."

Annie tried, but the puny snowballs she made kept falling apart in her hands. "Come here and help me, Alvin!" she shouted.

"In a minute," Alvin yelled through the falling snow.

"No! Right now!"

"Boy! What a pain!" said Marty. "I don't know how you stand it."

"Me neither, sometimes," Alvin admitted. "You'll just have to wait!" he shouted to Annie.

"But I need help!"

"You sure do," Alvin muttered. He left his snowball where it was and went over to Annie. He made a medium-sized snowball and put it in her eager little hands. "Now push it into the snow and roll it around so that it gets bigger and bigger."

"Then what?"

"Then you'll have the bottom of your snowman."

"Then what?"

"Then you do it all over again two more times and make the snowman's head and body."

"What about his eyes made out of coal?"

"I don't think there's any coal around here. You'll have to make his eyes out of potatoes or something."

Annie looked at the little snowball in her hand. "That sounds hard."

"Hey, come on," Marty shouted. "I'm doing all the work here!"

"Look, Annie," said Alvin. "I've got things to do. You've got your snowball. Do whatever you want." As he went back to rolling his snowball, Annie set hers down. She decided it was more fun to scoop up handfuls of snow and toss them in the air.

"This is a lot of work," said Marty, sitting on his snowball and surveying the situation. "We've only got two crummy snowballs so far. It's going to take us all day just to make one fort, let alone two."

"Yeah," said Alvin. "We really need a whole bunch of people to help."

"How about your Dad and Gramps?"

"Forget it," Alvin said. "They're watching the games all afternoon."

"Maybe we should, too. I'm getting cold. That wind can really sting you."

"Hooray for winter!" shouted Uncle Walt. Whooping and hollering and jumping up and down, he burst through the front door with Mom and Aunt Irene right behind him.

Uncle Walt romped through the snow and pointed to the snowballs. "What are those for?"

"A snow fort," said Alvin.

"You've got a long way to go," Uncle Walt observed.

"You want to help us?" Marty asked.

"Nope! I'm no warrior. I'm an angel!" Suddenly he fell backward in the snow and waved his arms up and down.

87

Mom and Aunt Irene laughed. "When we used to do that, you'd say it was for little kids!"

"Little kids and old men like me!" said Uncle Walt. He got up carefully, so as not to spoil Angel Walt's imprint in the snow. Then he ran up to Alvin's mom and pushed her backward. "Your turn!" he shouted.

Mom fell down and made an angel while Uncle Walt chased Marty's mom. Aunt Irene put up a good fight, but Uncle Walt pushed her into the snow, too.

"That's my mom's good coat," Marty said. "She's gonna be mad." But Aunt Irene seemed to be having just as much fun as her brother and sister. Alvin had never seen a group of adults act quite this silly before. It was almost as though they were just tall kids.

"Your turn!" cried Uncle Walt, lumbering through the snow toward Alvin and Marty.

"Forget it!" Marty said. "You were right. That's for little kids."

"You're no fun," said Uncle Walt, coming closer.

"Maybe not," said Marty, "but I'm not going to be some dumb angel."

"Well, Annie is!" shouted Uncle Walt. "Right, Annie?"

"Right!" she said. Uncle Walt gave her a little shove, and she fell over backward in the snow. Then she flapped her wings.

"How about you, Alvin?" said Mom, getting up from a glorious impression of an angel and brushing the snow off her coat.

"Oh, why not?" Alvin said, and fell backward in the snow.

"That leaves only you, Marty," said Aunt Irene.

"No! Forget it! I don't even believe in angels!"

"Make a devil, then!"

Marty thought about it for two seconds. Then he fell on his back in the snow. When he got up, there was a big round imprint. Right at the top he dug out two big horns. Everybody laughed and applauded.

Uncle Walt looked around the yard and began rubbing his gloves together. "There sure are a lot of angels around here! But you know what?"

"What?" said Annie.

"It's cold!"

"You said it," said Mom. "Are you kids warm enough?"

"I guess so," said Alvin.

"Will you make me a snowman?" Annie asked Uncle Walt.

Uncle Walt waved his arms over Annie's head. "Poof! You're a snowman!"

Annie pouted. "You know what I mean!"

"I haven't the foggiest idea," said Uncle Walt in a goofy voice. "And I am going inside to have a nice warm cup of tea."

"Good idea," said Aunt Irene.

"Maybe I'll make some cocoa," said Mom. "Are you kids going to come in?"

"I think we'll stay outside a little while," said Alvin.

"Not for real long, though," said Marty. "That cocoa sounds good to me." It sounded pretty good to Alvin, too.

"Okay," said Aunt Irene, "but if you start to get chilly, be sure to come inside. That wind's getting pretty fierce." Laughing, she and her brother and sister clomped through the snow and back inside the house.

"Boy, they're sure in a good mood," said Marty.

"I'll say," said Alvin.

"Make me a snowman!" Annie said.

"If we're not going to use these snowballs for a fort," Alvin said to Marty, "I guess we could turn them into a snowman."

"Yes! I need a snowman!" Annie insisted. She tossed some snow at Alvin and Marty.

"Watch it, little squirt," Marty said. "You may just find yourself getting some of this back."

"Will not!" said Annie, pushing more snow in Marty's direction.

Alvin had seen it before: when Annie got frustrated at not being able to keep up with bigger kids, she turned exceptionally grumpy. "Annie, don't get into one of your little cranky fit moods."

"Make me a snowman!" Annie cried. "Please?"

Marty whispered something in Alvin's ear. Alvin smiled and nodded. "One..." said Marty, "...two... *three!*"

And suddenly they both bent down, gathered up huge armfuls of snow, and dumped it all on Annie. "You're a snowman!" they shouted in unison.

Alvin knew it was a dirty trick to play on Annie, but he just couldn't resist. Standing there all covered with snow like a little pink shrub, she was a hilarious sight. But from the look on his little sister's face, Alvin realized exactly what would happen next.

Annie let out such a howl that anyone who didn't know better would have thought she'd been mortally wounded. Tears streamed down her cheeks. She ran up to Alvin and hit him in the leg. "Come on, Annie," said Alvin. "You're okay."

"No, I'm not," she wailed. She hit Marty, who just laughed. Then she ran through the snow and back to the house as fast as her legs could carry her, which wasn't exactly like lightning.

"Now we're in trouble," said Alvin. "I'm not supposed to do stuff like that to my little sister."

"It was hilarious," said Marty. "Why not?"

"Because she's too little, and she can't fight back."

"That makes it even better."

Alvin suddenly remembered that Marty hated baseball and cheated at games and broke toys without even apologizing. Alvin hoped creep germs weren't contagious. "I'd better see if she's okay," he said, starting toward the house.

"Not me," said Marty. "It wasn't my idea."

Between her tears and the snow, Annie had stumbled all the way to the house, so Alvin was able to catch up with her as she went through the front door. The house smelled wonderfully turkeyful inside. Faint footbally sounds were coming from the den. And suddenly Annie stopped her shrieking.

She had spotted the extra remote control on the hall table where someone had left it. Her wet footprints stained the carpet as she dashed to the table and picked up the control.

"Put that down, Annie," Alvin said, stopping in the vestibule to take off his boots so he wouldn't leave tracks on the rug.

"No!" cried Annie. She pushed a button. Cheers from the football game roared into the room.

"You might break something."

"No, I won't," said Annie. "Besides, you dumped snow all over me." She pushed the button again. Loud rock music replaced the football sounds.

"I'm sorry," said Alvin. "I apologize. Now give me that remote control."

"No." Annie pushed another button. The doorbell played "Over the River and Through the Woods."

"Annie, you might even mess up the turkey or something," said Alvin as he took off his other boot.

"No, I won't," said Annie. She made the doorbell play the song again.

"Annie, just put that down."

"No!"

Alvin dashed toward Annie. She stood her ground and defiantly pressed a button.

Suddenly the whole house became very still. All the lights went off. The doorbell, the lamps, the TV—everything quit, all at once, all through the house.

"Uh-oh," said Annie.

15

"What's going on?" Gramps hollered from the den. "The TV just quit!"

"So did the oven!" said Mom in the kitchen.

"Now you've done it!" Alvin shouted at Annie.

"I didn't do anything!" Annie cried, and ran away.

Alvin followed her to the kitchen. "Even the fridge has stopped," Aunt Irene was telling Mom and Uncle Walt.

"Mom, Alvin threw snow all over me!" Annie cried.

But before Mom could answer, Dad and Gramps and Grandma came in from the den. "What are you doing with that, Annie?" Dad asked sternly, pointing to the remote control.

"She was messing around with it," Alvin said.

"Alvin threw snow all over me," said Annie.

"Annie, did you play with that remote control?" Dad demanded.

"A little," Annie admitted.

"Hand it over," Dad said.

Annie did.

"This probably isn't anything serious," Gramps said. "I'll take care of it in a jiffy." He left the room.

Dad stooped down to Annie and waggled his finger right under her nose. "Annie, you were very bad."

"Alvin threw snow all over me."

"Did you do that, Alvin?"

"Sort of," Alvin said.

"You're supposed to protect your sister, not attack her," Dad said in a stern voice. "And as for you, Annie, you're supposed to listen when we tell you not to do something. I don't know what I'm going to have to do to punish you two."

"How about no turkey tonight?" Mom suggested.

A shiver rolled down Alvin's spine. No Thanksgiving turkey would be just about the worst punishment on the planet. He was pretty sure his parents wouldn't go through with it, but you never could tell.

"We'll just see," said Dad. "If these two step out of line again, it's no turkey for sure. And maybe even no dessert."

Alvin felt another shiver. Grandma's pumpkin pie with ice cream and whipped cream on top was another thing he couldn't stand missing out on. He should never have listened to Marty, that creep.

Gramps came back muttering under his breath. He went into the den and brought the other remote control back into the kitchen. He pressed some buttons on both controls and pointed them both at the ceiling. Then he pointed them at the floor. He fiddled with the light switches, he fiddled with the switches on the stove, and he fiddled with the switches on the electric juicer. He felt the heating panels. He picked up the telephone. Nothing worked at all.

Marty came in from the front of the house. "What's all the fuss about?"

"Annie was fooling around with the remote control, and now nothing works," Alvin said. "Even the lights are off."

"The stove, too?" Marty asked.

Alvin nodded.

"Annie, you broke the house!" Marty screamed. Annie burst into tears and ran away.

"Marty, that wasn't nice at all," said Aunt Irene.

Marty just shrugged. "She did, didn't she?"

Gramps was still fiddling with the remote control. "Maybe it's a circuit breaker that broke," he suggested.

"I knew you shouldn't have let Annie even touch that thing," said Dad. "Once she gets an idea in her head, there's just no stopping her."

"Oh, I'm sure she didn't mean any harm," said Gramps as he took a flashlight from a cupboard.

Alvin couldn't believe it. If he had broken his own house, especially by doing something he'd been told not to, Dad would've punished him for a month. But Annie had just broken this house, and Gramps was acting as though it was no big deal. When things went wrong, Annie always seemed to wriggle off the hook somehow.

Dad and Gramps put on their coats and headed out the back door. Since Alvin and Marty still had their coats on, they followed close behind.

Gramps brushed the snow from one corner of the porch and bent down to pull on a big iron ring. "It's a trapdoor!" Alvin exclaimed as Gramps yanked on the first door Alvin had ever seen that opened upward from the floor. In the doorway at his feet, he could see a set of stairs that led down to the cellar.

"Careful now," Gramps said, and Alvin quickly realized what he was talking about. The stairs creaked with every step, and the ceiling was so low it would be easy to hit your head. Cobwebs were everywhere.

"This looks like some old horror movie," said Marty, and it was true. At the bottom of the stairs was a dank, dark, cryptlike hallway that had the musty smell of damp wood. Cobwebs draped the wooden beams that supported the house, and the walls were lined with rakes and hoes and bushel baskets and other strange items that looked as though they hadn't been used for years. It was really neat in a spooky way. Alvin was almost glad Annie had fooled around with the remote

94

control, because otherwise he might not have seen all this.

The circuit breakers were in a tiny room off the main hallway. Dad held the flashlight, Gramps checked things out, and Alvin and Marty watched a spider scurry across the wooden ceiling. "Everything down here seems to be fine," said Gramps. "I wonder what that granddaughter of mine did to the system."

Dad sighed. "Leave it to the little mischief-maker."

"Back upstairs, everybody," said Gramps. "I'll get to the bottom of this!"

"Aren't we already at the bottom?" Alvin wondered.

Everybody groaned. "Save the terrible jokes for your Uncle Walt," said Gramps. "Now up those stairs, and don't bonk your head!"

Alvin went first. When he climbed back onto the porch, he thought he heard a faint voice calling, "Hello, over there!" But the storm was at its height now, and Marty said he didn't hear any voices. Alvin decided it was probably nothing but the wind.

"We've even got trouble out here," said Gramps. He pointed to the snow sticking to the electric sidewalks, which were now as cold as the rest of the yard.

Then Alvin heard it again. "Hello, there!" hollered the voice. It was coming from what looked like a bear lumbering through the backyard. But when the bear got closer, Alvin could see it was really just an enormous human being in a big fur coat.

"John!" Gramps yelled at him. "You got any electricity?"

"I was going to phone and ask you the exact same question, but the phone's dead!" the man hollered back.

"Sounds like a blackout to me," said Gramps.

John stepped onto the porch and shook his big bearded head in agreement. "Sure does. Good thing I had my Thanksgiving dinner already."

"Had your turkey at lunchtime, did you?" Gramps said.

"Turkey? Not me. I hate turkey. I just fixed up a mess of pork chops. That's my idea of a feast. These your relatives?"

"They sure are," said Gramps, and he introduced them all to John, who Gramps said was the finest plumber in the entire United States and possibly the world. John said he was pleased to meet them.

"Come on in awhile," said Gramps.

"No, thanks," said John. "I'd better get home. If this lasts awhile, I may be getting a lot of calls about frozen pipes and heating systems. See you all. Happy Thanksgiving, I guess." Everybody wished him a happy Thanksgiving as he trudged back into the storm.

"Wow!" said Marty as everyone went back inside. "A real blackout!"

"This is neat," Alvin agreed. "Have you ever been in one before?"

"Only for about half a minute in a thunderstorm once. How about you?"

"Not really. I've read about them, though. You have to have candles and flashlights and everything. Maybe it'll last awhile."

"It had better not last," Gramps said as he took off his coat. "If it does, you won't get your turkey."

"Huh?" said Marty.

"The oven's electric," said Grandma. "If we don't get our electricity back, we won't be able to finish cooking the bird."

"No turkey?" cried Marty.

"No stuffing?" cried Alvin.

"And no mashed potatoes with gravy, either," said Grandma. "I did make the cranberry sauce ahead of time."

"Who ever heard of cranberry sauce without turkey?" Marty demanded. "That turkey smells all right now. Maybe we can eat it just the way it is!"

"It's still almost raw," said Aunt Irene. "It went in only a little while ago."

97

"That's terrible!" said Alvin.

"You, sir, may not get your share of the bird even if it is cooked," Dad reminded him.

Alvin just stared at the floor. He didn't feel all that great about what he'd done to Annie in the first place, and he didn't like being reminded of it in front of everybody. Especially when it also concerned not getting to eat his all-time favorite food.

"Maybe we should listen to the radio to find out how long this is going to last," Aunt Irene suggested.

"Good idea," said Grandma.

Gramps reached for the remote control, pressed some keys, and pointed it at the ceiling. Then he realized his mistake. "Oops," he said sheepishly.

"You know," said Dad, "what we need around here is a thing of the past."

16

"We haven't used our old portable radio in quite a while," said Grandma. "I hope I can find it." And she went upstairs to search.

Mom looked out the window. "It sure is blowing out there."

"And it's going to get dark pretty soon," said Aunt Irene.

Alvin looked through a different window: the window of the oven, where the turkey sat in all its half-baked majesty. "Boy, just looking at that bird makes me hungry."

"I can't even stand to look," said Marty.

Grandma returned, radio in hand. "I found it, all right," said she. "I just can't seem to get it to work. Anybody got a quarter?"

Alvin reached for his lucky quarter, and then he remembered where it was. And he'd left his new lucky quarter upstairs in his other pants. Fortunately, Uncle Walt swept his arm around the room and magically discovered a quarter behind Marty's ear. "Amazing the places you find money these days!" he said, handing it to Grandma. "Don't spend it all in one place."

"I'm not going to spend it at all," said Grandma. "I need it to open the back of this darned thing to see what's the matter with it."

She turned the quarter in a little slot, and the back

of the radio snapped off. Out popped four batteries with flaky chemicals all over them. "Done for," said Grandma.

Gramps sighed. "I always check the flashlights. Wouldn't you just know I'd forget the radio?"

"And of course they take different-size batteries," Dad remarked.

"They certainly do," said Grandma, "and we don't have any of these." She dumped the old batteries in the garbage bin and washed her hands.

"Well, now what?" Marty asked.

Alvin had a brainstorm. "Why don't we use the car radio?"

"Alvin, that's really using the old noodle," said Uncle Walt. And to emphasize the point, he miraculously produced an old noodle from his left nostril.

"Okay, Alvin," said Gramps. "Come on out there and keep me company. Marty, you want to come, too?"

"Not me," said Marty. "I'm going to save my energy, just in case the power doesn't come back on and we have to starve."

Alvin and Gramps put on their coats and headed for the garage. By now the snow was higher than the tops of Alvin's galoshes. He walked in Gramps's footsteps to keep from getting snow down his boots, but even so, the wind blew some in, and he could feel it melt with a cold, wet tickle.

Inside the van, Gramps turned the key and turned on the radio. Out came a syrupy version of "Let It Snow, Let It Snow, Let It Snow."

"Let it stop," Gramps grumbled, "and tell us something about what's going on. At least they're on the air."

"Why don't you change the station?" Alvin suggested.

"We don't have the choice you do back in Sherwood Forest," Gramps explained. "This one's the only station right here in town. If it's just a local blackout, they may be the only ones to report it."

The song ended. A woman's voice said they had just heard "Let It Snow, Let It Snow, Let It Snow" and a bulletin about the blackout would follow this important announcement. The important announcement, which was accompanied by Annie's current favorite song, "Over the River and Through the Woods," was that the friendly folks at Engberg's Appliance Shop wished a happy Thanksgiving to all their friends in the tri-state area and reminded everyone that the store would be open late every shopping night until Christmas.

"Now the latest word on the power outages and the blizzard," said the announcer.

"About time!" Gramps snorted.

"Spokesmen for the local power authorities advise that a severe ice storm has created an electrical outage that extends for a radius of approximately fifty miles, centered just west of Tyler. Telephone service is also affected throughout much of this area. Service may not be restored until as late as tomorrow morning."

"There goes the turkey," Alvin sighed.

"Shhh," said Gramps.

"Blizzard conditions will continue through the evening. Accumulations of as much as eighteen inches are possible, and high winds will cause severe drifting and deep snowbanks. Drivers are urged to avoid all highways, and all residents are urged to avoid the frigid wind and sub-zero windchill conditions. Tomorrow will be sunny but cold."

Gramps shook his head.

"Residents are advised to use battery-powered devices such as flashlights wherever possible, and to take special precautions when using candles, fireplaces, or wood stoves to avoid the possibility of fire. Keep your radio tuned to this station, Nice 104, for the latest developments. We are operating with a special emergency generator and we'll keep you informed of all the latest developments."

Alvin sighed. "I wish *we* had a special emergency generator."

Gramps turned the radio off. "I guess we've heard the worst. Let's go in and break the news."

Alvin and Gramps tramped through the snow back to the house. "What's the story?" asked Aunt Irene.

"The story is, there won't be any power till maybe tomorrow morning."

"You didn't happen to hear how that football game was going, did you?" Dad inquired.

Gramps shook his head.

"I think I'll go out there and try to find it on the radio," said Dad, pulling on his coat. "This is the biggest game of the year."

"Until next week, anyway," laughed Uncle Walt.

"Don't freeze out there," said Mom. "They can probably win without your help."

Dad gave her a dirty look and went out the door.

"Forget about football!" said Marty. "What about the turkey? Some Thanksgiving this is turning out to be!"

"Let's all give thanks that things aren't any worse," said Aunt Irene.

"Worse? How could they be any worse?" Marty demanded.

"You could be out on the road, stranded in the middle of the storm," said Grandma. "You could be in some country where they don't even celebrate Thanksgiving."

"That's right," said Uncle Walt. "We may not have any turkey, but we still can have fun."

"Fun, my elbow," said Cousin Marty.

Alvin felt pretty much the same way. Thanksgiving without turkey was worse than the Fourth of July without fireworks. There had to be a way to cook the turkey. There just had to.

102

"Wait a minute!" said Alvin. "I just got another great idea!"

"Shoot," said Gramps.

"What if we roasted the turkey in the fireplace? They do that in *Little House on the Prairie* or some other book I read."

"Now, that *is* a great idea!" said Marty.

"A terrific idea," said Uncle Walt. He took a light bulb from his pocketful of tricks and pressed it against the top of Alvin's head. It lit up like magic. "This lad has one hundred watts of brainpower."

"There's one little problem," said Grandma. "We changed the fireplace over when we won the contest. If you look closely, you'll see the logs are fake. The fireplace is electric, too."

Alvin slapped his forehead. Not even million-watt brainpower could save Thanksgiving now.

"When is turkey time?" Annie asked as she came through the door from the dining room. She'd been upstairs playing with Lambie and her coloring books since the ruckus began, and she didn't know anything at all about how Thanksgiving had just been sabotaged.

"There isn't any turkey," said Marty. "And it's all your fault."

"Come on," said Alvin. "It wasn't really her fault. Don't tease her like that."

"Why not? There's nothing else fun to do around here."

"Is he kidding about the turkey?" Annie wondered.

" 'Fraid not," said Gramps, and he explained the blackout to her.

"What are we going to eat, then?" Annie demanded.

"I guess we'll have to starve," said Gramps.

"I'm not gonna starve!" said Annie.

"Well, I did see some cornflakes in the cupboard," said Gramps.

103

"Cornflakes!" Annie cried. "That's not Thanksgiving food! That's not even dinner food!"

Uncle Walt opened the cupboard behind him. "I see a can of chili here," he said.

"But the electric can opener won't work," said Grandma.

"I've got a can opener on my Swiss Army knife," said Marty.

"But you don't have any way to heat things up," said Uncle Walt. "It'll be chilly chili!"

"Chilly chili!" Annie made a face. "Yuck!"

"All right, everybody!" Grandma declared in a serious voice. "Enough joking! No more complaints! Nobody's going to starve around here. The refrigerator is full of food, and it's all delicious."

"Like what?" Annie demanded.

"Never you mind, now," said Grandma.

"But it's not turkey," said Marty.

"Now, don't be so sure, young man," said Grandma.

"But you just said we can't eat that turkey."

"I may just have a few surprises up my sleeve," said Grandma. "Now everybody out of this kitchen! Gramps and I have dinner to fix—so out of here till we do!"

The other adults asked if they could lend a hand, but Grandma told them no. "When Grandma says everybody, she means everybody," said Gramps. "Shoo, skedaddle, vamoose. O-u-t. Out!"

"I still say we won't have turkey," said Marty.

"And I say you may just have to eat your words—along with the turkey. Now out! And don't come back till I say it's suppertime."

On his way through the dining room, Alvin noticed the centerpiece in the middle of the long table. It was a festive bowl of colorful gourds and multicolored Indian corn. And right in the middle was an orange crepe-paper turkey. It seemed to be smirking at all the foolish humans in the U.S.A. who were planning to make a real bird the centerpiece of their Thanksgiving tables.

104

17

"There's nothing to do around here," Marty complained as they entered the living room. "We can't watch TV, we can't listen to the radio, and we can't even play records. All we can do is sit around."

"Now just one little minute," said Gramps. "What do you think people did before TV and radio and records and electric light bulbs?"

"Sat around and got bored, I'll bet!"

"They did not," Gramps replied. "We didn't have all this electric stuff when I was your age, and we didn't think life was so terrible. We read books out loud. We told tall tales and ghost stories. We did all kinds of things. And the first thing we'd better do before it gets any darker is find the candles and get them lit."

Alvin and Marty and Annie helped Gramps take the candles and candlesticks down from the hall-closet shelf. They put some in the bedrooms and some in the living room and some in the dining room. But when Alvin started to take candles into the kitchen, Gramps said, "Didn't you hear your grandmother? Nobody else is allowed in the kitchen but me."

"What's the big secret?" Alvin asked.

"Curiosity killed the cat," Gramps mumbled.

"Shhh! Lambie might hear you," Annie scolded.

"It's just an expression," said Gramps. "It means Little Miss Fussbudgets should keep their pinkies off things they're not supposed to touch. Now, no peeking while I go into the kitchen."

"I'm gonna peek," Annie said with a giggle.

Gramps sighed. "Annie, haven't you had enough trouble for one day?"

Annie put her thumb in her mouth. Gramps raced into the kitchen and back so fast there wasn't even time to try to guess his deep dark secret.

Everyone followed Gramps back into the living room. When he lit the candles, a warm, flickery glow filled the room.

But the room wasn't really warm at all. "It's getting chilly in here," Aunt Irene pointed out. "What are we going to do about heat?"

"I knew I shouldn't've let them put in that electric fireplace," said Gramps.

"With that wind outside, this house is going to cool down fast," said Mom. "It's not just going to be chilly in here, it's going to be downright cold. So right now, while it's still not too bad, we should put on sweaters and coats and mittens."

"We've got a lot of spare blankets and comforters upstairs, too," said Gramps. "Now's as good a time as any to rustle them up."

First everybody put on coats, and Uncle Walt covered his bald dome with a knit hat that said BIG BRAIN. Then, with the help of Gramps's flashlight, Alvin and Annie and Mom climbed the stairs to the top floor. Gramps opened the door next to Alvin's bedroom. Through the doorway was an attic crammed to the rafters with old junk.

"There's a sled!" Alvin said as Gramps's flashlight glinted off the runners.

"I knew there was one around here somewhere," Gramps said, moving toward two big wooden chests on the floor. "Hold this," he told Alvin, handing him the

106

flashlight. Alvin kept it pointed at the chest while Gramps lifted the heavy lid.

A cloud of dust rose up from it. Gramps bent down and brought out a big patchwork quilt with fancy diamond patterns in bright colors. "My mother made this," Gramps said.

"I remember that one," said Mom. "It used to be on Irene's bed. It's beautiful."

"It sure is," said Gramps. "Mom was the finest quilter for miles around. Here's another one." And he brought out a quilt with a pattern even fancier than the first.

"It stinks," said Annie.

"Annie!" said Mom.

"Well, it does," said Annie. "It smells awful."

Gramps took a whiff. "It does, at that. Old mothballs. We'll air these out awhile till we need them." And before Alvin knew it, he and Mom and Annie were laden down with blankets and comforters and quilts. Then, as everyone turned to go back downstairs, Gramps noticed something else. He took the flashlight and stood on tiptoe to bring down something dusty from the top of a tall shelf.

"The old picture albums!" Mom exclaimed. "I haven't seen those in years!"

"Wow!" said Annie. "Are there pictures of you in there?"

"Wait till you see," said Gramps. "Your mother looked a lot like you when she was a little girl."

"Was she cute like me?" Annie wondered.

"I sure hope not," said Alvin. He was positive Annie made a face at him, but it was too dark for him to see it.

They went downstairs to the second-floor landing and spread out the blankets and quilts to air. Then Gramps dusted off the picture albums and took them down to the living room, where Uncle Walt was practicing his repertoire of animal sounds.

"I want to see the pictures!" said Annie.

"Oink, oink," Uncle Walt snorted.

"All right, Little Miss Fussbudget," said Gramps. He sat down, lifted Annie up to his lap, opened the big book, and pointed the flashlight toward a faded brown picture of a boy in a cowboy suit. "Do you know who that is?"

"Is that my friend Franklin?" said Annie.

"Nope," said Gramps. "Marty and Alvin, you take a guess." He showed them the photo.

"Beats me," said Marty.

Alvin thought it looked a tiny bit like his grandfather. "It's not you, is it?"

"It most certainly is," said Gramps. "That picture is over sixty years old."

"That's old," said Annie.

"Did you have electricity back then?" Marty asked.

"I'm not *that* old," Gramps said. "Of course we had electricity. But we didn't have TV or radio or tape recorders or loud rock amplifiers. See that picture there?"

Alvin and Marty nodded. It was a picture of a bunch of people standing around a kitchen.

"Now, those are my father and mother and my sister," he said. "See that?" Gramps pointed to a big kitchen appliance. "You probably think that's a refrigerator."

"Isn't it?" Alvin asked.

"That, my friend, is an icebox."

Marty shrugged. "Same difference."

"Not at all. That was a *real* icebox. It wasn't electric. The iceman delivered a big block of ice that went inside the refrigerator. By the time it melted, you'd have a big pan of cold water to empty, and then the iceman would come around again."

"Are you kidding?" asked Marty.

"Scout's honor," said Gramps.

"Did you have those, too, Mom?" Alvin asked.

"Nope. Everything was electric by my day."

"But we can remember when TV was only black-and-white," said Aunt Irene.

"And when milkmen delivered milk fresh to your door in glass bottles," said Uncle Walt, offering his finest impersonation of a cow.

Alvin and Marty and Annie lay on their bellies on the floor and looked at the old photo albums. Alvin couldn't believe how much had changed over the years: back when his parents were growing up, cars were different, clothes were different, even haircuts were different. He decided his favorite picture was the one of Grandma and Gramps looking about as old as his mom and dad did now. Mom was a kid about his age, and she wore a frilly dress with gloves and a hat. And she was sticking her tongue out at the camera.

Annie liked that one, too. She could stick her tongue out with the best of them, and she demonstrated for the rest of the group.

Dad came in looking rather glum. "Did they win?" Mom asked.

"It's getting too cold to stay there and find out for sure," Dad said. "But they're losing by thirty to three in the last quarter, and Renfrew broke his toe."

"Did you hear any more bulletins about the blackout?" Gramps asked.

"Pretty much what you heard before," Dad said. "They did say it's the worst Thanksgiving storm in fifty years."

"So forget about the turkey, right?" said Marty.

"That's the general idea," said Dad.

"Anybody hungry?" asked Grandma from the hallway.

"We're starving!" said Marty.

"Well, good. Here are a few appetizers to tide you over till the meal." And she set a big tray down on the coffee table.

There were more than just a few. There were pickles,

109

olives, carrots, cherry tomatoes, cheese and crackers, breadsticks, and stuffed mushrooms. And then she brought in big bowls of potato chips, taco chips, and dips.

"Maybe you won't starve, after all," Gramps told Marty.

"How much longer till dinner?" Marty wondered.

"Twenty minutes or so," said Grandma with a wink. "Want to make sure the turkey's done."

"Very funny," Marty grumbled.

"Wait and see, Mr. Smarty," said Grandma, and went back toward the kitchen. But Alvin was as sure as Marty that the only turkey this Thanksgiving would be the paper one on the dining-room table.

Everybody took a napkin with a turkey or a Pilgrim on it and heaped a plate with food. "Okay, folks, watch this!" said Uncle Walt. "Alley ... *oop!*"

He tossed an olive high in the air and caught it right in his mouth. "Don't get them started," said Aunt Irene, but it was too late. Alvin had to try it, and so did Marty, and of course Annie got into the act. Each time Uncle Walt did it, the olive went straight into his mouth. But when Annie or Alvin or Marty tried, the olive bounced off a nose or chin or eye or missed altogether and ended up on the floor.

"Just as well," said Uncle Walt. "A friend of mine nearly died from choking trying this trick."

Next Uncle Walt used cherry tomatoes to demonstrate his juggling skills. First he juggled two, then three, then four, then five, then six. He was pretty good, too; they all seemed to be in the air at once, and he didn't drop a single one. "You know, Walt, we really don't encourage our kids to play with their food," said Mom.

"Sorry," said Alvin's trickster uncle. One cherry tomato after another landed in Uncle Walt's mouth and vanished forever.

"Dad, do we have extra batteries for the flashlight?" asked Uncle Walt.

"Plenty of 'em," said Gramps.

"Well, then, you're in for a treat," said Uncle Walt. And the next thing everybody knew, the wall came alive with his shadow puppets of everything from monkeys to butterflies, not to mention rabbits, ducks, and mosquitoes. He tried to teach them to the kids, but Marty wasn't interested, the only thing Alvin seemed to be able to get right was the barking dog, and Annie's animals looked more like waving hands than anything else.

While Uncle Walt was arranging his hands to portray an eagle in flight, someone created an amazingly lifelike silhouette of a cat, right down to the whiskers. "I've been beaten at my own game!" Uncle Walt cried, reaching down and hoisting the interloper to his lap. "Lambie, you do the most realistic shadow picture of a pussycat it has ever been my pleasure to see!"

18

Almost before anyone knew it, Grandma uttered the magic words: "Dinner is served."

"We will now have a candlelight procession," said Gramps. "Everybody but Annie, please bring a candle into the dining room."

"Why not me?" Annie demanded.

"You know you are not allowed to play with fire, young lady," said Dad.

"No, I'm not allowed to do anything fun," Annie grumbled.

In the flickering glow of the candles, the long table and big lace tablecloth in the dining room looked like something out of an old-fashioned movie. The table was set with fancy flower-design plates, fancy mono-grammed silverware and glassware full of curlicues, and fancy napkins with scenes from Pilgrim days. Grandma had made turkey-shaped place cards for everyone, and Alvin found his between Dad's and Uncle Walt's.

And there was food! Platters full of cold cuts, bread, and rolls nudged big bowls of coleslaw, pickled beets, cranberry sauce, and salad. Grandma brought in all the appetizers from the living room. There were fancy glass pitchers of milk and soda pop for the kids and Aunt Irene, and bottles of red and white wine for the rest of the grown-ups. Only one thing kept it all from being perfect.

"See, I told you," said Marty.

"Just hold your horses," said Grandma. "Now dig in, everybody."

"Wait!" said Dad. "I want to propose a toast. To a dinner we should all be thankful for, and to many more besides."

"Hear, hear," said Uncle Walt.

And everyone raised his glass and clinked it with everyone else's. Even Annie got into the act, and though she spilled some of her milk, nobody seemed the least bit upset about it.

Alvin wasn't quite sure where to start. He was particularly curious about how the cranberry sauce would taste with stuff that wasn't turkey. He decided to make himself a sandwich out of the cold cuts and bread and cranberry sauce and sample a little of everything else until he decided what he liked best. The trickiest part was eating with his winter coat on and making sure he didn't dip his sleeve in beet juice or something.

"We've even got a candlelight dinner," said Gramps. "In the fancy big-city restaurants, you pay extra for that."

"Now remember, everybody, save room for dessert!" said Grandma as she watched the food disappear without any help from Uncle Walt's magic.

"I knew there wasn't going to be a turkey," Marty grumbled, but Alvin noticed Marty seemed to be doing quite well with what was on the table. Even without the turkey, there was so much food that it wasn't hard to overeat.

Everyone talked about the wind and snow howling outside the windows and wondered when the blackout would be over. Grandma and Gramps told stories about storms of their childhood. They said the worst part about this would be that nobody would get to take a bath.

"No bath?" shouted Annie. "Hooray!"

"No something else, either," Marty griped.

Uncle Walt waggled his finger at him. "Some people," he said, "can have a pile of donuts in front of them, but all they see are the holes."

"I don't see any donuts," Annie said. "Where are they?"

But everybody else knew what Uncle Walt meant. Alvin thought Marty really was being pretty obnoxious. Alvin missed the turkey every bit as much as his cousin did, but after all, the blackout wasn't anybody's fault, and Marty was probably making Grandma and Gramps feel rotten.

After everybody else had seconds and Alvin and Marty had thirds and Uncle Walt began to make groaning noises, Grandma said, "Now, nobody else get up. Gramps and I are clearing the table all by ourselves, and that's final."

Mom and Dad and Aunt Irene tried to get up and help, but Grandma and Gramps shooed them away. "Just mind your own business," said Grandma. "Everybody relax and stay put."

So Alvin's grandparents cleared the table themselves, and everybody joked that they seemed to have something up their sleeves. But when they came back, all they had was dessert—scads of it.

There were three pies: pumpkin, mince, and apple. There was a big chocolate cake. There were cookies in the shape of Pilgrims and turkeys and pumpkins. There were special candies that looked like Indian corn. But, as Marty put it with his best I-told-you-so look, "There's still no you-know what."

As if that were his cue, Gramps gave a slightly off-key fanfare on an old cornet. Then Grandma came through the kitchen door with something that looked amazingly like—Alvin couldn't believe it, but yes, it was—a turkey! In the dim candlelight Alvin could see the golden skin, the succulent wings, and the meaty drumsticks. Juices actually seemed to be dripping from the thighs. Everyone gasped at the sight.

"I don't believe it!" Marty exclaimed.

As Grandma set the turkey down on the table, a piece of the drumstick seemed to melt. Annie was the first to notice. "It's ice cream!" she cried.

"Can't fool you, Little Miss Sharp-Eyes!" said Gramps.

"How in the world did you do that?" Mom asked.

"Well, if the blackout lasts much longer, everything in the freezer will turn to mush," Grandma said. "So I thought, why not put some of those sculpture classes I've been taking to good use and give it a try?"

"It's beautiful, Mom!" said Alvin's mom. "I'm going to get my camera."

"Forget about the camera!" said Marty. "The bird is melting! Let's eat."

"Marty, you owe your grandmother an apology," said Aunt Irene.

"I apologize. But I still say let's eat!"

"Now you know you're not going to starve," said Gramps. "And Alice wants to record this bird for posterity."

Mom took one picture of the turkey on the table. She took one of Grandma holding it up proudly on its platter. And she took one of everybody smiling at it, except for Uncle Walt, who made a silly face and pretended to attack it with his knife and fork.

"Now can we eat?" Marty whined.

"You'd better!"

Gramps carved this turkey with a spoon. Grandma had made the skin from orange sherbet, and in just the right places there was dark and white meat—chocolate and vanilla. But what Alvin liked best was the stuffing: rocky road. The melting ice cream made delicious gravy.

Alvin had a little of every dessert: three different pieces of pie, one piece of cake, four cookies, and a handful of candy. But even though this turkey didn't come with mashed potatoes and it wouldn't be very good left over the next day, Alvin liked it the best of all.

Grandma insisted that everybody pitch in and finish the turkey on the spot. "If you don't," said she, "it'll just turn into turkey soup."

Some of the adults protested and patted their stomachs and said they were too full to eat another bite. But Alvin and Annie and Marty did their best to help. By the end of the meal, all that remained of the most unusual turkey ever was a little orange-and-brown-and-white puddle.

19

There may not have been a genuine stuffed bird, but nine genuine stuffed human beings waddled into the living room after the meal. Uncle Walt performed his best card tricks. Grandma and Gramps taught everyone the words to a bunch of old songs Alvin had never heard before. And Lambie batted at the fringe that dangled down from one of Grandma's oldest chairs.

That night, for the very first time in his life, Alvin slept with all his clothes on, including his winter coat, his knit cap, and his gloves. When he went to bed, he could actually see his breath, but beneath a thick down comforter, two blankets, and a quilt, he was warm and toasty. He was also slightly jealous of Marty, who got to use a big sleeping bag downstairs.

Annie forgot all about asking Alvin to finish the bedtime story from the night before and fell asleep in a flash. Alvin went right to sleep, too. But just as he began dreaming of giant turkeys on the warpath, alarms suddenly started whooping, music began blaring, and electric light blazed forth in every room in the house.

Annie woke up in a fright with Lambie in her arms. "I didn't do it, and neither did Lambie! Honest!"

"Hooray!" Alvin shouted. "The power's back on!"

"Are the lights on up there?" Gramps hollered up the stairs.

"Yes!" Alvin shouted.

Suddenly the whole top floor went dark again. "No!" he shouted. "Not anymore!"

"Same here! False alarm, I guess!" Gramps shouted back.

"See?" said Annie. "It wasn't my fault at all."

At five in the morning, the alarms and the music and the lights came on again. Annie cried, "False alarm!"

But it wasn't. This time the lights stayed on for good, and Gramps went around the house adjusting things with his remote control. Grandma called everyone downstairs to sit around the electric fireplace and drink homemade cocoa. Then peace descended upon the house again. And warmth: Alvin could hear the heaters crackling into action, though it was still so cold he had to sleep in his coat.

By the time Alvin woke up for the third time, it was late in the morning and gloriously clear outside. The cloudless sky made even the snow look blue.

And there was snow aplenty. There was too much for the electric sidewalks to handle, so with Gramps's thing-of-the-past show shovels from the attic, Alvin and Marty dug the walks out, helped dig out Aunt Irene's car, and moved on to work for some of the neighbors.

Marty somehow seemed to stick Alvin with the hardest jobs, but Alvin didn't complain. Together he and Marty made almost twenty-five dollars until some kids with snow throwers and trucks with plows came by and stole their business. Even Gramps hired a plow to dig out the wide driveway. "I'd love to give you the job," he told Marty and Alvin, "but you have to be back in school Monday morning."

Late that afternoon, Alvin and Marty finally made

118

Annie her snowman, complete with apple eyes and carrot nose and walnut smile. On his way inside for cocoa, Alvin thought he smelled a familiar aroma wafting through the house. One peek through the oven door confirmed his nose's suspicion. There, getting browner by the minute, was a huge, glorious turkey! That night at dinner, nobody could decide which bird had been the bigger success.

But as Alvin was getting started on his third portion of turkey and stuffing, all the lights suddenly went off. "Oh, no!" said Gramps.

"Not again!" cried Marty.

"I didn't do it!" Annie wailed.

Then, with a great flourish, Uncle Walt made the remote control appear out of thin air. With one press of a button, everything came on again.

"No dessert for you, Walter Montoon!" said Grandma just the way Mom said it when Alvin had done something wrong.

Uncle Walt just chuckled and magically conjured up a cookie.

On Saturday, everyone went to the shopping mall, and Annie waited in line to see Santa Claus, even though a certain cousin made snide remarks about it. Alvin and Marty fooled around with some expensive toys they didn't really want. They ate pizza, shish kebab, and tacos, and washed it all down with frozen yogurt. On the way back to the house, they noticed that the adults were toting some mysterious Christmassy packages that everyone else was forbidden to look at.

The hardest part of the trip was saying good-bye, except to Cousin Marty. Uncle Walt gave Annie and Alvin rubber pencils that looked exactly like the real things. Then Grandma and Gramps drove them to the airport, where they exchanged big hugs and told all the Hooples to stay well.

"And, oh, yes," said Gramps, slipping Alvin a little envelope with something wadded up inside. "This is for you." The outside said DO NOT OPEN UNTIL YOU GET HOME.

The flight back wasn't nearly as interesting as the one going out. Alvin didn't make the metal detector beep, he didn't get to sit right next to the window, he didn't get stuck in the bathroom, and he didn't even spill salad dressing all over his shirt. But he did get to see the cockpit. And the envelope drove him crazy with curiosity every minute of the flight.

On the way to the airport parking lot, Dad suddenly stopped and looked around. "Where did we leave the car, anyway?"

"I don't remember," said Mom.

"Do you, Alvin?" Mom asked.

"Not me," he said, giving Annie a dirty look. "I was worried about keeping that cake in one piece."

"We went around the lot so many times," said Dad, "that it all began to look the same. I thought it was around here somewhere. I should've written it down."

"I remember!" said Annie.

"You do not," Alvin declared.

"I do too!" said Annie.

"I bet!" Alvin said.

"Okay for you, Mr. Smarty! The car was right near the sign with the big seven! Seven comes after six!"

Annie and *Sesame Street* had come through in a pinch. Everyone gave her three cheers.

As the car pulled onto the highway, Alvin felt the envelope in his pocket again. He decided being in the car was really the same as being home. So he opened the envelope. Inside was a ball of cotton, and inside that was a quarter from the year he was born. A key ring was attached to it. And a note said, "As long as you keep this, you'll never be broke. Love, Gramps."

Alvin felt terrific. He couldn't wait to get back home and put his keys on his new lucky-quarter key ring and phone his friends and tell them all about the greatest Thanksgiving ever. He felt so good he hardly minded at all when Annie kept singing the first line of "Santa Claus Is Coming to Town" to Lambie over and over again.